WHAT YOU DON'T SEE

Two lives. One story they never saw coming.

A Hidden Battles Novel

AYNDE NUKARA

Contents

Dedication

To my children, who are my greatest joy in life.

To my parents who did the best they could in a very different generation.

To the parents who journeyed with me in the early years of our family's autism, ADHD, EDS hypermobility, PDA and DCD diagnoses. Especially the small few who have characters very loosely based on them in this book.

Thank you for inspiring this book and for your role in me becoming who I am today.

To the Autism Community at large. It is impossible to truly portray the diversity of autistic representation in one book or series and I have chosen to focus on what I have lived in my own life. As such you may not see yourself in these characters especially if you are gender diverse. I hope that this can still be a step forward for all autistic people including you.

Prologue

Mickey

I never meant for the blog to become a thing. Honestly, it started as a place to vent so I wouldn't yell at strangers or cry in public — two activities I try to limit to once a week. But then people started reading it. Sharing it. Quoting it back to me like I was some kind of emotionally unstable fortune cookie.

And somewhere along the way, my friend Angela — who has the subtlety of a marching band — asked if she could use a few of my stories for a parent support group she was running.

I said yes, mostly because I assumed no one would actually listen. Shows what I know.

What I didn't realise then was that those late-night ramblings — the ones I wrote to stay sane — would eventually help a cocky Texan ex-hockey player named Jace stumble into the best friendship (and love story) of his life.

And no, he wasn't looking for love. He was barely looking for sleep.

A tragedy had knocked Jace sideways. His career was on pause. And his brother — over in Perth, ten thousand miles from the ice rinks of America — was quietly falling apart as his marriage imploded. Liam had always struggled to connect, and Anna had always been the one who made the world make sense for him. So when she moved out and Liam finally broke enough to ask for help, Jace did the only thing he could. He got on a plane and went to Australia.

Within hours of landing — despite old knee and pelvis injuries screaming at him — he took his nephew out so Liam and Anna could try to put themselves back together.

And that's where this story begins: with an act of family duty, a jet-lagged uncle, and a little boy who needed more than anyone realised.

I didn't know any of this at the time. Back then, I was just trying to survive my own life without spontaneously combusting. But I share it now for the same reason I shared my blog:

Because stories bring healing. And laughter. And hope. And sometimes the reminder that you're not the only one who feels like a malfunctioning human Roomba – one of those robot vacuums that bumps into everything and somehow makes things worse despite its programming.

People think adventures come with plane tickets, exotic locations, and narrow escapes. But sometimes the greatest adventure is learning to be your honest self — and embracing the honest selves of the people who crash unexpectedly into your orbit.

Don't get me wrong — there are trials ahead. Not the cinematic kind with swords and prophecies, but the real kind: the ones that test your patience, your courage, and your ability to keep a straight face when everything goes sideways.

There will be toy bananas. There will be glitter slime. There will be fixations, meltdowns, breakthroughs, and enough coffee to power a small nation.

There will be moments that feel like tightropes, detours that feel like labyrinths, and escapes that hinge on timing so precise it borders on miraculous.

But that's the thing about adventures — they're rarely glamorous. They're messy, human, and unexpectedly transformative.

If you're here for something neat and tidy, you've taken a wrong turn. But if you're here for something messy, funny, brave, and unexpectedly life-changing?

Well. You're in exactly the right place.

Chapter One

The Stranger Who Calmed the Storm

"Storms are just seasons to endure; you prep, you brace, and you don't let them take what matters — especially your happiness."
Mickey's Blog Bits

Jace

The second I pull into the shopping centre car park, my brother Liam's voice blasts through the rental car speakers like he's trying to shout across the whole damn Pacific. My knee aches from the long flight from Texas, my hip's stiff from sitting too long, and my attention keeps snagging on the wrong things — the rattle in the trunk, the heat shimmering off the hood — instead of the actual conversation.

"Buddy," I say, dragging a hand down my face. Jet lag's chewing on my brain, the Perth heat's finishing the job, and my thoughts are bouncing around like loose change in a dryer. "He's a five-year-old kid, not a wild bull. We're almost there."

"You went the way I told you?" I hear him ask.

"Yes," I say, leaning into the drawl because it annoys him. "I followed your sacred banana trail. And I told him we'd get bananas. You said bananas calm him, right?"

"He loves them, but—"

“I can handle this,” I say, softer this time, trying not to let the frustration bleed through. I’ve just stepped off a thirty-two-hour flight, and I offered to take my nephew Harry to the shops so Liam could talk to Anna alone. I don’t get his panic — his wife moved out three weeks ago, he barely sees her, and all Harry has done since I walked in is stare at my hoodie like it’s the most interesting thing in the room.

Not at my face. Not even close. His eyes keep drifting to the drawstring, the zipper, the stitching near my shoulder. Tracking movement. Fixating on details. I don’t know what that means, but it’s... different. The kid’s studying me without actually looking at me.

“Go meet with your wife,” I tell Liam, steady but firm. “Y’all need to sort this out for Harry’s sake.”

I forgot to add the bit about how I’m here now — how he asked for help and I came — but maybe he already knows. Or maybe he’s too wound up to hear it.

There’s a long, shaky breath through the car speaker.

“Call me if—”

“I will,” I cut in, because if I don’t, he’ll spiral and drive straight back here.

I hang up and twist around in my seat.

Harry sits in his booster, staring out the window, legs swinging, fingers tapping a rhythm on his thigh like he’s playing invisible drums. He still doesn’t look at me — but that’s okay. I’m new. Everything is new.

“Hey, little man,” I say gently. “You ready to grab some stuff? Then we’ll get bananas and head home.”

No reaction.

I smile anyway. “Love the enthusiasm.”

I get out, walk around, and unbuckle him. He steps out, still not looking at me, but he takes my hand when I offer it. His palm is warm and a little sweaty — the kid’s got a grip like he’s holding on through a tornado.

As we head toward the entrance, a woman pushing a trolley slows down, smiling at Harry.

“Oh, he’s adorable,” she says brightly.

Harry keeps walking, laser-focused on the automatic doors like they're the gates to Narnia.

I grin at the woman beside me. "He knows. He's just selective about who he shares it with."

"Yours?" she asks, giving me the look — the *'you taken'* one.

I give her my usual charming smile, the one my long-term ex Mel used to roll her eyes at. "No kids, darlin'. He's my nephew." I've always been a flirt. Mel hated it. I'm not a player — not in that sense.

She tries to keep up as I follow Harry, but I shut it down. She reminds me of Mel — copper hair, slim, tall. Attractive, sure, but if I'm honest, I prefer curves.

"Sorry, miss. I need to catch up with my nephew — first time looking after him." I offer a feigned, disappointed smile.

She laughs. "Good luck."

"Thank you, ma'am." I give her a quick half-bow. "I'll take all the luck I can get."

Inside, the shopping centre hits us with a wall of noise — voices, trolleys, some store blasting music like it's auditioning for a nightclub. The air smells like coffee, floor cleaner, and cinnamon scrolls that should honestly be illegal.

For ten minutes, everything is fine. Harry keeps checking where I am — or at least I assume that's what he's doing when he glances back at my legs. He seems to know exactly where he's going, and we're not in a rush, so I let him lead. We weave between the checkouts and the aisles as if we're on some kind of mission.

Then he turns his head again, eyes flicking to my pant leg. "Nuh, nuh." He points down the freezer section.

Thank God for the pointing — and the shopping list. For a second I thought he was trying to say *banana*, but Liam said he uses a **/a/** like *apple* for that, and this was definitely a **/u/** like *umbrella*. So it had to be something else.

Look at me. Already nailing the kid-speak.

We head toward the freezers.

Cold air blasts out like a blessing from the heavens. I open the door and twist to grab the nuggets; my hip twinges — the same damn spot I injured playing hockey years ago. It's fine. Just a war wound.

Before I can adjust—

A baby shrieks behind us. Sharp. Sudden. Loud enough to rattle my teeth.

Harry suddenly looks like he'd been holding it together all this time — the chatter, the trolley wheels, even the music — but the baby's cry is a different frequency. Sharp. Sudden. It slices through whatever calm he had left. He drops my hand, his hands fly to his ears. His breathing sharp. His eyes wide.

"Hey, hey—" I reach for him, but he bolts.

"Harry—!" I blurt out as I drop the nuggets back into the freezer and slam the door shut to chase him—

Except my shirt gets caught.

The door yanks me back so hard I nearly kiss the glass.

"Oh, come on," I hiss, wrestling with the freezer like it had personally offended me. The freezer door has apparently decided we're in a committed relationship.

I tug. It tugs back. I twist, my hip screaming at the angle. The freezer twists my shirt tighter.

"Let go of me, you frosty demon," I mutter, sounding like a man being manhandled by a disgruntled baby yeti who definitely woke up on the wrong side of the glacier.

I finally rip myself free. Slip on a patch of melted ice. And do a half-split that would've ended my sports career all over again.

I make a noise that is absolutely not a whimper.

And recover. Barely.

Then sprint after Harry.

I turn the corner—and skid to a stop.

Harry is sitting on the floor, arms curled around his knees in the far corner, rocking, eyes squeezed shut, soothing himself with each sway back and forward.

And kneeling near him is a woman.

She holds a small yellow toy — a banana — and breathes in slow, predictable rhythms.

Not dramatic. Not intrusive. Just steady.

The kind of anchor that doesn't demand anything from him. Harry's rocking slows, then stills, drawn to the pattern.

Her voice is soft, barely a ripple in the surrounding noise.

She doesn't touch him. Doesn't reach for him. Just breathes — slow, steady breaths, like she's trying to calm the whole damn aisle.

Harry's rocking stops.

He inches toward her, eyes locked on the toy.

I stay back. Whatever she's doing... it's working. Better than anything I've managed all day.

Then I actually see her.

Long, wavy brown hair with curls that look like they've got opinions. My attention snags onto her before I can stop it. Curves that make my jet-lagged brain short-circuit. A quiet confidence that hits me harder than the Perth heat.

I see the soft smile she gives him and feel myself longing for it to be aimed at me.

Lord help me.

Harry reaches her. She holds out the toy banana.

"Here you go," she murmurs, Aussie accent warm and soft. "You can keep it mate."

Harry takes it instantly.

I step forward, trying to look like a man who has his life together. "Hi. I'm Jace. This is my nephew, Harry. Thank you. Seriously."

She looks up at me with a blank, unreadable expression.

"Oh. Okay," she says, glancing at her watch. "I'm late. Gotta go."

That's it.

No smile. No "you're welcome." Just a nod.

She stands, brushes off her jeans, and turns to leave.

I blink. "Uh—"

Harry tugs my pant leg and raises the banana. “Na-na.”

I crouch down so we’re eye-level. “Yeah, buddy. You did great. That was a lot, huh?”

He doesn’t look at me, but he presses the toy banana to his cheek for a second — a tiny, soft gesture that knocks something loose in my chest.

I smooth his hair back gently. "That is a cool banana," I say softly.

He leans into my hand for half a heartbeat before straightening again. It’s small. But it’s real. And it hits me harder than the jet lag.

“Alright,” I say, standing and guiding him toward the fruit section. “Let’s get you some real bananas.”

As we walk, a woman smiles at Harry. “He’s gorgeous.”

I catch the glint of interest in her eyes, but my head’s still back in the aisle where that other woman knelt down and somehow calmed him. Whoever she was, she did more in ten seconds than I managed in ten minutes.

Harry keeps walking, determined.

I grin. “He’s got priorities.”

She laughs and heads off in the opposite direction. My eyes follow her longer than they probably should. I give my head a quick shake and look down at Harry again.

I look down at Harry again — at the way he clutches the toy banana, at the determined little set of his shoulders — and something warm settles in my chest.

“Na -nas,” he says softly.

“Bananas,” I echo. “And maybe... maybe we’re gonna be okay.”

Chapter Two

The Strengths They Can't See

"Use the wrong tools to understand someone and you'll miss every strength they have. The problem isn't the child — it's that we haven't learned how to listen."

Mickey's Blog Bits

Kayla

I managed to get here just on time, after getting held up at the shopping centre, but it didn't calm my nerves any. Parent Teacher interviews are never fun, not as the teacher and not as the parent, but I would rather be the teacher in this case. My son is in Education Support, a school for disabled children and you would think that this would mean that they understand him right? This is the third year he has had this teacher, once in year 1, then again in Year 3 and now in year 4. She cares I know she does, but I just don't think she and my boy are a good combination.

"He is refusing to do any of the assigned work."

The teacher's voice is careful — the kind of careful that has been practised. I catch the rehearsed cadence immediately, the way her sentences line up like bullet points. My brain warns me she's about to list his behaviours instead of his needs, and I feel myself brace for impact.

"He has multiple methods of avoidance — leaning over the desk, leaving his seat and roaming around the classroom, staring into space, trying to get the education assistant to play instead, requesting food, asking to go to the toilet but not needing to go."

I nod once, jaw tight. The fluorescent light above us buzzes wrong, threading itself through her words and making them sharper than they need to be.

"This isn't good for him or the other students when he's behaving this way."

A small, tight breath catches in my chest. My thoughts sprint ahead — a dozen explanations, a dozen corrections — but I keep them behind my teeth.

Part of me wants to bring up that behaviour specialist who visited the school last term. The one who said the teacher stood in front of a developmentally delayed Year 3 class and talked about space with a PowerPoint for thirty straight minutes. I want to say that I'm an intervention teacher, that I've spent years working with traumatised kids who are more complex than my own son, and I do it without support. I want to say that I can get those kids learning, connecting, laughing — yet somehow an entire school can't seem to bring out the best in Archie.

I shouldn't be judgemental. But it's hard to fathom why they can't do this.

I've learned the hard way that saying too much in these meetings only makes people defensive. And I need processing time to form an argument, to build my script. As much as I hate it, I know I have to try.

"He is intelligent," I say instead, voice steady. "He knows how to get people to do what he wants. He knows how to hide his actions. I know he's non-speaking, and it's hard to determine what he understands. I just want to give him the best opportunities."

A tremor starts in my body, but I hold my posture. I keep repeating my words in my head.

I did well. I didn't go too far.

The teacher softens, but only slightly. "I know he is more capable than he is showing. We will do our best, but I need to be honest with you about what we're seeing in the classroom."

I swallow. "Thank you."

The meeting ends with polite smiles and a stack of papers that feel heavier than they should. I step outside into the bright schoolyard, blinking against the sun. The air smells like warm wood chips and the dry, clean bite of eucalyptus drifting in from the trees.

I look for the duty teacher who said she'd watch Archie during the meeting. She's over by the play equipment with the other kids, keeping an eye on everything. When she spots me, she points across the yard and smiles.

I follow her gesture and see Archie immediately — sprawled in the grass near the big gum tree, lying flat on his back like he's sunbathing. A soft smile tugs at my mouth. His hands float above his face, twisting and circling in slow, mesmerising patterns. His head sways gently from side to side, a soft, rhythmic movement. A quiet hum vibrates in his throat, steady and soothing.

"Archie," I call gently. "Come on, sweetheart. Time to go."

He doesn't move. His fingers keep dancing in the air, tracing invisible shapes only he can see. His hum shifts pitch, then settles again.

I try again. "Archie. Up we get."

Nothing.

I sigh — not frustration, but surrender. I walk over, crouch beside him, then finally give up and lie down next to him on the grass.

The world tilts. The sky fills my vision — wide, blue, endless, peeking out from the eucalyptus branches shading us. Archie lies beneath them, his hands drifting through the air like he's conducting light. His head still sways to a rhythm only he feels. His breathing is steady. Peaceful.

I watch his fingers swish and curl, and something inside me loosens. The tension from the meeting — the words refusing, avoidance, behaving this way — begins to ebb away.

My thoughts race anyway.

"Archie... what is the right thing to do for you? Am I pushing you too much? The world doesn't see your intelligence — not the way I do. But am I demanding too much from you just so they'll see it?"

I close my eyes.

I just want to give you everything I can. It's hard to step back and let things happen in your time. You're not like Violet — she pushes herself, I have to stop her from being too hard on herself. But you... if I didn't nudge you along, you'd just watch the world go by.

A breeze rustles the leaves above us. Archie's fingers flutter faster, then slow again, syncing himself to the wind.

I turn my head toward him. "I love you," I say softly. "More than anything. I just want to support you. I'm trying. I hope I'm doing it right."

Archie suddenly turns his head toward me, eyes bright, and says, "Tickles."

I blink. “Tickles?”

He nods, very serious. A tiny foot wiggle runs through his body — anticipation.

I huff a laugh — the first real one since I walked out of the classroom — and reach over to wiggle my fingers against his ribs.

Archie squeals, kicks his legs, flaps his hands, and laughs so loudly a couple of kids on the oval turn to look. His joy is full-bodied, unfiltered, pure.

I laugh too, the sound surprising me with how light it feels.

For a moment, the meeting doesn’t exist. For a moment, the future doesn’t exist. For a moment, it’s just the two of us, lying in the grass, the sky above us, and Archie’s laughter shaking the world back into something I can hold.

Chapter Three

Brothers, Bruises and the Truth We Avoid

"Bleed yourself dry and you can't support yourself, let alone anyone else."

Mickey's Blog Bits

Jace

Harry falls asleep in the car on the way home, banana toy clutched to his chest like it's the crown jewels. I carry him inside, his head heavy on my shoulder, and push the door open with my hip.

Voices hit me immediately.

Not shouting.

But sharp. Tight. Controlled in that way couples get when they're trying not to let the neighbours hear.

"...you're not listening to me, Liam—"

"I *am* listening, Anna, I just don't agree. When are you moving back in? Is this really worth breaking our family apart?"

"Liam, if I don't take care of myself, I can't take care of anyone else. It's not selfish — it's necessary."

I step into the living room just as Anna turns. Her face softens instantly when she sees Harry.

"Oh, *mein Schatz*," she murmurs, taking him from my arms. She presses a kiss to his forehead, whispering something in German that sounds like comfort and exhaustion braided together.

Harry stirs, sees her, and melts into her shoulder.

"We're going to visit Onkel Heinrich," she tells him gently. "He has the good biscuits."

His eyes flick to the yellow banana toy. Anna notices it, smiles, and brushes her thumb over the tag.

I tense — expecting questions. But she just nods, like it makes perfect sense.

"*Banane*," she says softly. "Of course."

Then she exhales — a thin, frayed sound — and whispers to Harry, "Sorry, baby..." And under her breath, barely audible, *"Ich kann nicht mehr."*

The German slips out so naturally it takes me a second to place it. Anna's German-Australian, but she only sounds German when she's frustrated or overwhelmed. I asked her about it once and she laughed, saying that in those moments she channels her Oma — the great matriarch of her family, born in Germany and immigrating to Australia in 1958, shortly before giving birth to Anna's father.

Anna told me once that her Oma never raised her voice, but when she was pushed to her limit, she'd switch languages mid-sentence, muttering sharp, efficient German phrases under her breath while she powered through whatever crisis was in front of her. "German is for when things need to get done," Anna had said, smiling.

I haven't heard that accent in years. The fact that it's back now tells me everything I need to know.

She grabs her bag, adjusts Harry on her hip, and turns to Liam. Her expression shifts — not cold, just worn thin.

"We will talk later," she says.

Liam's jaw tightens. "Yeah. Sure. Drive safe."

The door closes behind them.

I turn to Liam. "Uh... *Ich... kan... nich... mer?*" I butcher it so badly it sounds like I'm chewing gravel.

He doesn't look at me, just mutters, "It means 'I can't anymore.'"

Silence drops like a curtain.

Liam exhales hard and collapses onto the couch. I sit beside him, and we stare at the AFL game on TV — two teams I don't know, doing things I don't fully understand.

"These guys are insane," I say. "You gotta be half mountain goat to play this."

Liam snorts. "Yeah. And half masochist."

We watch a few plays. A guy gets tackled so hard I feel it in my spine.

"Oof... that's gonna leave a mark," I mutter. "They don't wear any padding?"

"Nope," Liam says. "Just stupidity and pride."

I huff a laugh. "Respect. That's a brutal sport."

"Not as brutal as hockey," he says. "But close."

"Different kind of brutal," I say.

He glances at me. "You miss it?"

I don't answer right away. I haven't been on the ice in a year. Not since one of the players I coached was injured. He almost lost his life. Compared to what happened to him, all I can think about is how lucky I was that my injury wasn't more severe. I crave the ice, but I'm not ready.

"Yeah, the money was good," I say finally. "Helping the rookies improve, keeping them safe — that part mattered."

"So, it's just her," he says. "I know the breakup with Melanie messed you up, but it's been a year."

I groan. "Don't bring up Mel."

He shrugs. "She was a nightmare."

"She wasn't," I say, sharper than I mean to. "It was complicated."

Liam gives me a look — the *I've known you your whole life and even I know you're full of it* look.

He doesn't know the truth. No one does. Not about the post-traumatic stress disorder. Not about the aftermath of my injury. Not about the things I learned in hospital rooms and quiet offices. Not about the things I can't give anyone.

Mel thought I was overreacting because of the PTSD. Thought I was pushing her away because I was hurting. She never knew I ended it to free her.

"Whatever you say," Liam mutters. Then, quieter, "At least you had a choice."

I turn to him. "What's that supposed to mean?"

He rubs his face. "Just cause some friend of hers suggested he was like her kid who has autism. Anna wants Harry assessed for autism. I don't. I can't lose her but..."

There it is. The fight I walked in on.

"Why don't you want him assessed?" I ask carefully.

"Because he's fine," Liam snaps. "He's like me. He likes things a particular way. He likes to line things up in order. He gets stuck on stuff. He hates loud noises. So what? That's not a disorder — that's just... us."

I raise an eyebrow. "You hyper-fixated on building a model train set for six months and didn't even realise your girlfriend broke up with you."

He points at me. "I was a teenager and that was one time."

"It was three. Same girlfriend but three times."

He scowls. "Not the point."

"What is the point?"

He slumps back. "Anna thinks I'm refusing to learn. She wants me to go to some parent information group — 'A Cuppa Support' or whatever. Says I'm not helping her enough. Says I'm gone too much. Says she feels alone."

His voice cracks.

Just a little.

But enough.

I let the silence stretch.

Liam isn't dramatic. He isn't emotional. He's the kind of guy who says exactly what he thinks, even when it lands like a punch. But right now, he looks... lost. Like he's holding the world up with one hand and it's starting to slip.

"You two love each other," I say quietly.

He huffs. "Love doesn't fix everything."

"No," I agree. "But trying can."

He stares at the TV. We remain silent, focusing on the game. I know he avoids uncomfortable things, and I don't know what I have to offer that won't make it worse.

Another brutal tackle. Another roar from the crowd.

But one of the players is on the ground and not getting up. The game is halted and medics are cutting across the ground.

Liam winces next to me. He says something — probably a joke — but the words don't reach me.

A cold sensation slides through my veins, sharp and creeping.

My muscles lock.

I know what's coming, and I can't stop it.

The room fades before the memory even hits — colours draining, sound dulling, the edges of everything blurring like I'm slipping underwater.

I'm caught in the in-between. Not in the lounge room. Not on the ice. Just suspended in that unreal space where everything feels wrong.

Then the memory slams into me.

The hit. The boards. The crack. The pop. The warm rush down my leg. The panic. The helplessness. The sound of my own breath stuttering in my helmet.

I'm not fully in the memory anymore, but I'm not in the lounge room either.

I'm stuck — frozen — caught between two realities.

A hand grabs my shoulder.

"Jace. Jace — are you okay? Jace, answer me."

Liam's voice cuts through the fog, but the room still feels tilted, distant, unreal.

I plant my feet on the floor. Press my back into the couch. Dig my hands into my thighs.

And I breathe.

In. Out. Long and slow. Again.

Again.

A grounding trick the team chaplain taught me after the injury — when the nightmares were worse than the pain.

Slowly, the colours return. The TV noise filters back in. The couch feels solid beneath me.

Liam's face comes into focus — tight with worry.

My breathing steadies. My pulse slows.

"I'm okay," I manage, voice rough. "Just... got a bit lost."

Liam doesn't look convinced.

But he lets it go.

"So," he says after a moment, nudging me with his elbow, "you gonna tell me why Harry's holding a toy banana?"

I grin, grateful to be talking about anything else. "Oh, that? Some woman gave it to him."

Liam raises an eyebrow. "Some woman?"

"Yeah," I say, leaning back. "Long brown hair, curves that could cause traffic accidents, eyes like she could see straight into Harry... and she calmed him down in about ten seconds flat."

Liam snorts. "And?"

"And she ignored me completely," I say. "Didn't even blink. Just handed him the banana and walked off like I wasn't even there."

He laughs — a real one. "Mate, you lost your charm already? You've been in Australia for what, 8 hours?"

"Jet lag," I say. "Heatstroke. Emotional damage from fighting a freezer."

"Sure," he says, smirking. "Or maybe she just wasn't impressed."

I throw a cushion at him.

He catches it easily, still grinning.

And for the first time since landing in Perth, my world feels lighter.

Chapter Four

A Cuppa Support

"Every brain functions its own way. The trick isn't forcing them to match — it's finding the people who can tune into your frequency without asking you to change it."

Mickey's Blog Bits

Jace

Anna walks ahead of us into the community centre, shoulders tight, arms wrapped around Harry like he's the only thing holding her together. Harry is perched on her hip, giving his new banana toy a full commentary on the cartoon he watched before we left the house. The kid has a memory like a steel trap — I swear he remembers half the dialogue.

Liam steps forward before Anna even reaches the tables. "I'll take him," he murmurs, voice low but steady.

Anna hesitates — just for a second — then nods and lets Harry slide into Liam's arms. Harry goes willingly, head dropping onto Liam's shoulder, banana toy squished between them.

Liam adjusts his grip with the ease of someone who's done this a thousand times, even if he's only home half the month. FIFO weeks drain him — home feels too loud, too fast, too much — but he still tries. Harder than he admits.

He turns his head slightly toward Harry. "Dad will take you to the play area," he says, jerking his chin toward the divider.

Anna exhales — the first real breath she's taken since we left the house.

I follow them inside.

The room is nothing like I expected.

Two long conference tables have been pushed together to form one massive rectangle, big enough to seat sixteen people. Five chairs line each long side, three on each end. It's structured, organised — not the loose circle I imagined. A few parents are already seated, steaming coffees in hand, nibbling on snacks in the centre.

Mostly women. One man. No couples other than Liam and Anna.

Relief loosens something in my chest — at least I wasn't about to be the lone single guy crashing date night. I needed to be here if I wanted Anna to trust me with Harry's care, but I didn't want people looking up like I'd taken a wrong turn.

On one of the short sides, two women sit with a pile of papers between them. One has long reddish-brown hair with greying temples, round glasses, and a mug that reads *Chaos Coordinator*. Her fuller frame is professionally dressed compared to everyone else here in jeans and sweaters. She looks up as we enter.

"Anna," she says warmly. "Glad you made it. And you brought extra support today."

Anna gives a small, grateful smile. "Yeah. This is my brother-in-law, Jace. And Liam's here too — he's just taken Harry to the play area."

Angela beams. "Perfect timing. I'm Angela. We're just about to start. Please take a seat. We've got about ten minutes before we begin, so feel free to grab a cuppa and some snacks. Since we're all new here today, we'll start with introductions."

As she finishes, the other woman beside her looks up.

It's her. The stranger from the store.

My breath catches. My balance pitches for a second — like the warmth inside me flash-freezes, a sudden sheet of ice slicking through my chest.

What the hell is wrong with me?

I didn't know what I expected — but it wasn't this.

Anna places her bag near the stranger and heads off for coffee. I take a seat along the long side of the table, close enough to hear Liam's voice drifting faintly from behind the divider as he settles Harry in. A moment ago I'd felt reassured but seeing her now knocks something loose. I feel like an imposter here — like I've skated into the wrong locker room. My insecurities flare, the ones born from losing the part of myself that used to anchor me. But I'm here for Liam, for Harry, for Anna. That's what matters.

Anna returns with a coffee for herself and a tea for Liam. “Did you want anything, Jace?”

I shake my head, realising I'm still staring at the woman from the store.

Anna turns to look at her and seems to realise who she is because she smiles and says, "Hey Kayla, thanks for giving Harry the banana toy. I assume you saw Harry at the store with Jace."

Kayla says something, but I miss it — I'm too busy watching Liam lean in with that look he gets when he thinks he's figured something out. He'd come back, taken one glance at us, connected everything instantly, and now he was convinced it was his job to tease me about being ignored by my perfect woman.

I'm so grateful when Angela clears her throat to start the session.

“I'm Angela. I'm the facilitator for *A Cuppa Support*. I'm also mum to a daughter with cerebral palsy, and a professional chaos wrangler.”

Soft laughter ripples around the table.

“And,” she adds, gesturing to the brunette beside her, “this is Kayla. I asked her to attend the sessions as we have a high number of parents with autistic children. She has two autistic children — one with consistently high needs and low independence, and the other with fluctuating needs and higher independence. She provides lived experience and insight, while I keep us on track.”

Kayla gives a small nod. She looks up, smiles politely, then drops her gaze back to the table, fingers tapping lightly — a rhythm only she seems to hear. I'm doing everything in me to focus on something other than her.

Kayla

Angela starts the introductions.

My stomach tightens. Ice-breakers. The worst invention in human history. I start mentally drafting what I'll say — something short, something safe —

when I realise Angela has already introduced me.

Relief floods my chest. I look up long enough to acknowledge the room, then drop my gaze back to the table and tap my fingers lightly to steady myself.

Once Angela asks Anna to share, I know the attention is no longer on me. I sit up straighter and let my brain do what it always does in unfamiliar rooms: catalogue everything.

I can see Anna. She reminds me of Diane Kruger — beautiful, German, blonde, tough, but at the moment she's nervous, exhausted, lonely. Shoulders tight. A protective hand on her bag. Her eyes flick to her husband every few seconds. I've met her a few times now; I introduced her to Angela.

Next to her is her husband, Liam — tall, light brown hair, and built like an NFL player, but without the cocky jock swagger you'd expect from an American who looks like a linebacker. And yes, he's American, so the NFL comparison tracks.

He looks relieved when Anna introduces him, then immediately panicked when he realises he might still be expected to speak. His jaw tightens, his knee starts bouncing, and he scans the room like he's mapping out escape routes.

My social-anxiety buddy, apparently.

Jace — the ever-so-confident brother. Calm, steady, watching Liam more than the room. Very protective. It took me a moment to place him earlier, because I was overwhelmed by life the last time I saw him. He was the one in the shops with Harry — the man who came sprinting up, breathless and apologising, muttering about fighting with a freezer while I tried to calm his nephew, Harry. I barely registered anything beyond *flustered uncle; Harry needs the banana; and crisis contained.*

But now, seeing him properly, the rest of the memory snaps into focus. He was also the one with the smile and the dimples that made me almost forget I was late for an appointment.

He is handsome. Too handsome. And far too charming for my peace of mind.

Across the table, the rest of the faces are equally exhausted, equally nervous. They seem friendly. They listen carefully.

Behind the divider, the children play — happy, entertained. I hear every sound, every shift, every squeal. I hear the scrape of a chair, the clink of a mug, the rustle of paper. All at once. Always at once.

Something happens in the play area, and Angela pauses the introductions to help sort it out. I offered to go but it was an equipment problem, so Angela needed to fix it.

One of the parents across the table starts making jokes to fill the silence. People laugh.

I wish I could be funny like that.

My mind drifts to the metaphor that came to me this morning — the only way I've ever been able to explain my racing brain.

It's like there are four supervisors running the control room in my head. Not helpful supervisors. Not "teamwork makes the dream work" supervisors. More like the kind who got promoted by accident and HR lost the paperwork.

There is the socially anxious foreman, General Overthinker Owen. Serious. Structured. Loves a plan. He's got colour-coded scripts, three escape routes, and a laminated list of "acceptable human responses." He's the only one who thinks he's in charge, and honestly? Even he shouldn't be.

Then there are the triplets:

Overshare Olivia, who runs the emotional channel. She feels everything at full volume and narrates it like she's mic'd up for a reality show.

No-Filter Nancy, who runs the sensory channel. She's a hyperactive blurter. If a sensation hits, she reports it. If a thought appears, she says it. No delay. No discretion. No survivors.

And Factoid Frank, who runs the logic and knowledge channel. He's basically a walking "Did you know...?" generator with no sense of timing.

When they cooperate, it's lovely — a polite conversation, information flowing neatly, no one yelling.

Sometimes two talk at once and I can still keep up.

And sometimes... sometimes they all scream at once. Random stimuli. No order. No filter. Full sensory W.W.F. Nancy is body-slamming Frank, Olivia's prepping a clothesline like she's about to headline WrestleMania, and Frank is still trying to explain the physics of why this shouldn't be happening.

Usually, in public, Owen keeps them in line. But not always.

For example, take a party. Owen prepares for a week — what to wear, what to say, how to stand, how to escape, how to fake confidence, how to fake faking confidence. He briefs the others like he's planning Helm's Deep in an alternate-universe battle where the Death Star teamed up with Sauron — dramatic monologues, a battlefield PowerPoint no one asked for, and the absolute conviction that only three of us are making it out alive.

Then we arrive.

At first, everything's fine. The triplets behave. Owen is smug. He's mentally drafting his Employee of the Month speech.

Then someone asks a question we didn't prepare for.

All three triplets turn to Owen. Owen freezes — completely offline, like his brain just lost signal and is buffering in real time.

Before he can reboot, Olivia panics and starts improvising. Nancy jumps in with commentary no one asked for. Frank adds trivia like he's auditioning for a quiz show.

Five minutes later, Owen comes back online, horrified. Damage already done. Olivia, Nancy, and Frank shrug — "I didn't do it," they chorus, which is impressive, considering all three of them absolutely did it.

Owen curls into a metaphorical foetal position, mumbling that we're never recovering from this. The rest of the night spirals until the triplets finally get bored and agree to use one of Owen's escape plans — usually the one labelled "fake an early start tomorrow" or "sudden mysterious illness."

That's my brain. Well — the simplified version. A constant cycle of complex chaos pretending it can be wrangled.

I'm shaken from my thoughts as Angela restarts the introductions.

Liam's jaw re-clenches, knee bouncing so high it could be dribbling a soccer ball, while he scans for an escape. Yep — I'm definitely not the only one in the room with social anxiety.

But his brother seems to understand, and he starts, "Howdy, my name is Jace. I'm Liam's brother, an ex-hockey player, and while I'm off the ice, I've come to help my brother and his wife with my nephew Harry."

Nancy must have escaped Owen's watch because she is ogling Jace like he is the most handsome man on earth. Objectively, Frank would add that he is attractive and, well, my ideal type. Yes, I have a type; we are all allowed to be a little bit shallow, you know. He has dark brown hair, light olive skin, hazel eyes, and a lightly chiseled face.

Oh damn, no. That smile. The dimples. He is bad news. All charm and swagger. The kind of guy you know had to be popular — and had the ego to match.

I'm relieved when the next woman speaks because I can force myself to move my attention away from Mr. Charisma. Her build looks petite, but she is too tall — probably about 5'7" — blonde and beautiful with a model-like face.

"Hi. My name is Priya. I have three children. My eldest, Dale, is autistic; my middle child, Joshua, is my tornado; and my youngest, Thinley, is my 'normal' child," she says, wincing at the word *normal*. She looks more exhausted than any other parent in the room — you can see it in her posture, despite the defiance in her lifted chin. "My husband is useless," she adds. "Divorce pending."

There are a few nervous chuckles as no one is sure if she is serious or not. But for me, everything together — her tone, her resigned body language, and the grit of her facial expression — tells me she is serious.

A bright-eyed, bubbly brunette woman with restless hands and energy vibrating under her ivory skin cuts off the chuckles. "Always here for you, Priya. I'm Sarah. I'm Priya's friend. My son, Noah, has ADHD, but I've come because Angela said I would still get something out of this, and I can help Priya more if I understand all our boys better," she adds, turning to the man next to her as if announcing she has finished.

He is older but not old, maybe forty-eight. He has dark brown hair with just a couple of greys at the temples. His light brown eyes reflect a deep sadness — and something more. "I'm Tom. I'm looking after my grandson Arden, who was diagnosed eight months ago, just before his mother and father were killed in a car accident."

The room is silent, respecting the grief this man still clearly carries.

"I'm sorry for your loss," says the lady clutching a notebook just a little too tightly, hope and fear tangled in her expression. "I'm Janette. My daughter was diagnosed recently. I'm still learning what that means, and every time I learn something, I feel like I'm understanding my husband more." She says the last part with a cheeky grimace. She is a beautiful young Asian woman with a shiny long black bob, fair porcelain skin, and a petite frame.

I turn to the last woman here. Her spine is straight, her chestnut hair in a flawless bun, her dark blue eyes sharp, and it appears she has walls thicker than mine — but maybe she is just shy. "I'm Martha. I have two children: a son, Alex, aged thirteen and diagnosed with autism at eight, and a daughter, fifteen, diagnosed with autism quite recently. I understand my son's autism, but not my daughter's. They are very different."

The introductions conclude.

Anna's exhaustion. My social-anxiety buddy Liam. Jace's devilish charm. Priya's blunt, weary honesty. Sarah's sunshine-over-storm energy. Tom's quiet grief. Janette's nervous hope. Martha's guarded intensity.

Every word, every shift, every micro-expression — I store it all.

It's how I survive.

Angela explains the structure of the group. I already know the script, but I listen anyway.

"We will start with a life story related to the topic," she explains, "and we will follow that with comments, discussions, and questions."

"My friend Mickey, who writes a blog called *Our Autistic Journey*, has given me permission to use the life experiences from her blog. Today we are going to look at labels and diagnosis."

Chapter Five

The Weight of Words - the labels we carry

In the world of diagnosis, labels get a bad name, but they're really just identifiers. The trouble starts when people lack knowledge and attach the wrong ideas to the label. The spice cumin is a good example. It's often avoided, handled with extreme caution, or even despised — not because there's anything wrong with it, but because people misunderstand its value. The label isn't the problem. The perception is.

Mickey's Blog Bits

Angela reading Mickey's Blog

"Diagnosis Day" — please don't judge me

The waiting room was too bright. Too clean. Too quiet. My son was twenty-three months old, and I'd spent the whole morning pretending I wasn't terrified.
People had told me he might be autistic. Other people — mostly family — said, "He's too affectionate. He can't be."
The clinicians asked their questions, endless questions. He ignored them, eye contact was non-existent. He flapped and paced, occasionally banging his head or hands on the table. I tried to manage him while they continued questioning me.

Then they stepped out of the room to "discuss." That was the moment I couldn't escape the fear — sharp and electric. I was sure they'd come back annoyed. I was sure they'd say I was wasting their time. I was sure they'd ask why I even came. Instead, they said, "Yes. He is autistic. Level 3. Level 3."

I nodded like I understood. But I didn't. Not really. I'd worked with autistic kids, but I didn't understand autism the way he needed me to. So, I learned. I read. I watched. I listened.

Four months later, I read an article about autistic girls misdiagnosed with depression. And I knew — I just knew. Immediately I had my daughter assessed. Again, I wound myself in knots, expecting judgement. Everyone told me there was no way she was autistic and again — yes, she is autistic. Level 2. Level 2.

These are some of the rare times I'm grateful I'm stubborn enough to follow my gut, even when it scares me. I knew something the day I read that article — really knew it — even though it would take another two years before anyone else verified it.

That I was autistic. And if I was, then my mini-me daughter would be too.

I was diagnosed autistic. Level 2. Level 2.

My beautiful daughter and my amazing son are the only reason that today I finally understand why I always felt so different.

Kayla

The room stills.

I feel the shift — the collective inhale, the shared ache.
Half the people at this table have lived this story.
Including me.

A few wet eyes.

A heavy stillness.

Martha wipes her cheeks. "That... that was exactly how it felt for us."

Janette nods. "I felt the same fear."

Tom stares at the table, jaw tight.

Liam doesn't move.
His eyes are fixed on a random spot in front of him, but I can see the impact.

His hands are clasped so tightly his knuckles are white.

Angela looks around gently. “Would anyone like to share their experience?”

Tom clears his throat. “My daughter and her husband were told Arden was ‘just naughty.’ Took them three years to get someone to listen.”

Martha adds quietly, “My daughter masked so well the teachers said she was just shy.”

Across the table, Janette flinches at the word *masked* – we all know the damage too much masking can cause.

Out of the corner of my eye, I notice that Harry has escaped the children's area, he slams into Anna’s lap, almost knocking her off the chair. She steadies herself and him with one hand, still listening. She runs her hands through his hair in an effort to calm them both.

Liam seems lost in himself, unaware that Harry is there. He shifts, trying to make himself smaller despite his size.

Anna pulls Harry up into her lap, she starts to speak and then hesitates — torn between honesty and protecting Liam. “I’ve had people ask why I’d want to ‘label’ my son.”

Liam tenses.

Priya lets out a humourless laugh. “People love saying that. Before my son was diagnosed, he wasn’t ‘label-free.’ He was labelled rude. Spoiled. Difficult. Even my tornado, Joshua who hasn't been assessed yet, gets labelled – and most of those labels are negative”

Sarah nods, her usual brightness dimmed. “Before my son’s ADHD diagnosis, he was called lazy. Aggressive. Dumb. Those labels stuck harder than the real one ever did.”

A murmur of agreement moves around the table.

Angela leans forward slightly. “It’s interesting, isn’t it? People argue that avoiding diagnostic labels protects our kids... but the world doesn’t stay quiet. It fills the gap with its own words.”

My fingers tremble under the table, but my voice stays steady.

"Labels happen whether we choose them or not. The question is whether the label helps or harms. We all want to protect our kids. Sometimes the hardest thing is making decisions that come with both good and bad consequences — weighing up whether it's worth it."

Jace and Liam both glance at Harry, who is now lining up his sultanas with intense concentration.

I continue, "Like many of you, when my children were little, people had plenty of labels for them. 'Naughty.' 'Odd.' 'Too sensitive.' 'Too much.' The diagnosis didn't create labels — it replaced the wrong ones with the right one."

Martha nods. "Exactly. Without the diagnosis, no one took us seriously."

Tom adds, "And once we had it, doors opened. Support. Understanding. Even just... patience."

Janette's voice is small but earnest. "I didn't want a label for my daughter either. But the alternative was everyone assuming she was choosing to struggle."

I tap lightly on the table to steady myself. "A diagnosis doesn't change who they are. It just gives people the right language to understand them."

I pause, then add, "And yes, sometimes you'll have to correct misunderstandings and fight battles you never imagined. But often... the diagnosis is the only thing that gets your child what they need."

The room absorbs the words quietly.

I glance at Liam.

He's not breathing properly.
His shoulders are tense.
His eyes are fixed on the booklet like it might explode.

He's terrified of failing his son.

I know that look – I've felt that feeling.

When he looks up, I give him a quick, gentle smile — not lingering, not long enough to make either of us uncomfortable.

JACE

I watch Kayla — the calm, the certainty, the way she seems to understand the whole room without saying much.

And I think about the woman in the supermarket.

The one who calmed Harry in ten seconds flat.
The one who walked away before I could even ask her name.

There's something about her.
I don't know what — but something.

The session wraps up slowly — chairs scraping, cups clinking, parents murmuring as they gather their things.

But Liam doesn't move.

He sits there, staring at the booklet like it's a confession he wasn't ready to hear.

I know that feeling. I felt it for months after everything went sideways. The feeling of realising something you don't want to know.

Kayla stands, gathering papers. She doesn't look at him — not directly — but she gives a small nod in our direction, almost like an acknowledgement.

Liam's eyes flick up for half a second.

Half a second is enough.

There's something raw in his expression.
Something like fear of being seen.

He drops his gaze immediately, jaw tightening.

I place a hand on the back of his chair — not touching him, just grounding the space between us.

"You good?" I ask quietly.

He nods once.
Too fast.
Too sharp.

He's not good.

But he needed this.

And whatever happens next...
starts here.

Chapter Six

Lunch, Labels, and the Space Between

People think listening is about hearing words, but most of the important things people communicate never make it to sentences. Fear has a tone. Exhaustion has a rhythm. And overwhelm is a tidal wave that shows up long before someone can name it. Real listening isn't catching every word — it's about noticing the things a person hasn't found language for yet.

Mickey's Blog Bits

Jace

We were about to leave the group when Liam wandered off and Tom came over to ask me about hockey and whether I played any other sports. We talked for a few minutes before his grandson tugged him away. Nice guy. He reminded me of my old team chaplain — steady, gentle, the kind of man who listens more than he talks.

Liam returned, rubbing the back of his neck. "Anna asked if we want to grab lunch. I have to fly out to work again tomorrow, but I told her you could look after Harry when she works. I think she wants to make sure you'll be okay with him."

I heard him, but part of me was still back in that room — in the conversations, the honesty, the weight of everything those parents carried.

It felt like my brain was trying to rearrange itself around what I'd just learnt. I'd heard assessments were a big deal, but I'd never understood the fear behind them. The shame. The labels. The way a single sentence from an assessor could change the entire trajectory of a family.

I looked at my brother, and for the first time, I really saw him. The strain in his shoulders. The exhaustion behind his eyes. The way he was trying to protect his son with everything he had.

And I saw something else too — something I hadn't understood until today.

Why Anna was drowning. Why Liam was cracking. Why they needed me.

Anna was already seated when we reached the café table. She looked drained — not just tired but worn down in a way that made something in my chest tighten. This wasn't the woman I'd stayed with two years ago for Harry's third birthday. Back then she was colour and noise and movement. Liam used to call her his storm of sunshine.

Now she looked like someone weathering storms alone.

"Hey, Anna," I said as we sat down. "I'm happy to look after Harry whenever you need. I've got no work or plans for the next month. Just tell me what you need."

A tiny piece of the weight she carried seemed to lift. She exhaled, long and shaky, and started explaining Harry's routines — her hands moving in small, anxious circles.

"...and if you change something, you have to tell him first. Not just do it. He needs warning. And don't forget the banana toy — he'll look for it if he gets overwhelmed. Oh, and if he starts spinning, don't try to stop him, just—"

I reached across the table and touched her hand gently, enough to stop the anxious circling.

"Anna," I said quietly, "I'll follow the routine you've created. You can walk me through anything I've missed when I pick him up."

She blinked, surprised. Maybe relieved.

Lunch arrived. She barely touches hers.

Liam cleared his throat. "I don't want Harry labelled."

Anna froze. Her fork hovered mid-air. Her eyes closed — not dramatically, just... like she was bracing for impact.

"Liam," she said quietly, "we've talked about this."

He opened his mouth, but she kept going — and this time, she didn't hold back.

"You think I want this? You think I want strangers judging him? I'm doing this because I can't keep doing it alone. You're away for weeks at a time. My family can only handle him for half an hour before they hand him back. Friends have stopped inviting us anywhere. People stare when he melts down. They whisper. They judge."

Her voice cracked, but she pushed on.

"And when you come home, you don't follow the routines that keep him regulated. You undo everything I've put in place because it doesn't make sense to you. You like things a certain way. You always have. But Harry isn't you. He needs a different structure. Predictability. And when you change things without warning, he falls apart — and I'm the one picking up the pieces."

Liam's jaw tightened. Defense mode. Classic.

"Anna—"

"No," she said, shaking her head. "I'm burnt out. I'm trying so hard. I'm trying to keep Harry regulated, keep the house running, keep my job, keep myself from falling apart. And you... you're not supporting me. You're not trying to understand. You're sabotaging me without even realising it."

She wasn't yelling. She wasn't angry. She was just... done.

Liam swallowed hard. "Anna... I'm supporting Harry going for the diagnosis."

She blinked. Once. Twice. Like she wasn't sure she'd heard him right.

"What?"

"The things the group said today. Especially your friend Kayla..." He rubbed the back of his neck. "He'll be labelled whether I want him to be or not. People will make assumptions no matter what we do. But maybe this — the diagnosis — maybe it's our chance to understand what he can't tell us."

Anna's face crumpled — relief, not fear. Tears slid down her cheeks. Liam reached for her hand — awkward, hesitant — like he wasn't sure he had the right.

I stood, because whatever happened next was between husband and wife.. "I'm gonna hit the bathroom."

As I passed behind Liam, I leaned down and whispered, "It doesn't matter where we are — hug your wife."

When I glanced back, he was already moving around the table, pulling Anna into his arms. She folded into him like she'd been waiting years for that exact moment.

And watching them, it finally clicked.

Liam wasn't adaptive — never had been. He needed predictability, sameness, order. Anna was doing everything the way Harry needed, which was the opposite of the way Liam did things. She has to be adaptive, flexible, structured in a way that made no sense to Liam's brain.

She wasn't just juggling a child who needed more than most people could give. She was juggling a husband who couldn't understand why the things she did were the opposite of what *he* needed. And he wasn't trying to sabotage her — but he was. Constantly. Unintentionally.

No wonder they were both breaking.

I slid back into my seat once they'd settled, Anna wiping her cheeks, Liam staring at the table like he'd just realised he'd been holding a grenade with the pin half-pulled.

I kept my voice steady. Practical.

"Alright," I said. "Let's make a plan."

They both looked at me.

"Anna, tell me what days you're working and need me to take Harry. And add some days where you're not working — so you can actually have a break."

She stared at me like she wasn't sure she'd heard right.

"And Liam's been showing me everything you've created — the routines, the strategies, the supports. When Liam's home, I'll help him follow them, so he doesn't undo what you've built."

Anna's breath hitched — not a sob, just a release. Liam looked relieved. And for the first time since I'd arrived, the three of us felt like a family trying — really trying — to understand each other.

My family never really understood Liam's quirks when we were kids, but we loved him anyway. He was just... Liam. Rigid. Literal. Stubborn in ways that didn't make sense to anyone but him. It wasn't until I played with a teammate who was almost exactly like him — same need for predictability, same struggle to adapt to new plays — that it finally clicked. His brain didn't switch gears the way ours did. It wasn't attitude. It wasn't defiance. It was wiring.

After that, Liam and I got closer. Not in a dramatic way — just in the quiet, steady way where he'd come to me when he needed someone to translate him to the rest of the world. It didn't happen often, but when it did, I was the one he trusted to help people understand him.

Anna had always just... accepted him. She never questioned the way he was. I never imagined I'd be sitting here years later, trying to help *her* understand him too.

Chapter Seven

Dancing in Storms

I used to think joy needed the right conditions — calm days, tidy plans, everything under control. Turns out it also hides in the messy ones — the ones you never expected, never scheduled, and definitely never dressed for.

Mickey's Blog Bits

Kayla

The Therapy Centre looks like a warehouse from the outside — plain walls, high roof, no hint of the chaos hidden inside. Violet leans forward in her seat as we park.

"Why are we going to this, Mum? You don't usually go out on weekends."

She's right. I don't usually go out on weekends unless it's a family event.

"Mrs. Moore asked me to come to the fun day for the parent group I help her with. There are kids close to your age and Archie's age. She thinks it might be good for us socially."

Violet nods, suddenly excited. I must have forgotten to tell her about the other kids. Honestly, I think Angela is doing this more for me than for them. I accidentally told her the last time I met up with friends was a year ago. I forget other people find that weird.

I step out of the car into a light breeze. It's cool and grounding for half a second before the nerves kick back in. Archie follows, trying to shut his door. He's getting better but still can't get the force right. I close it for him.

He's in a great mood today, which should calm me, but it doesn't. Part of me almost wishes it were a bad day, so I'd have an excuse not to be here. When you're brought into a group to give expertise, it's hard to build friendships. People see you as a walking resource, not someone worth knowing. It's the 5th session for this parent group and even I have to admit, they are very friendly and I feel like they try to get to know me and not just my knowledge.

We started with Labels and Diagnosis, then we looked at autistic socialisation and processing. Week 3 we examined communication differences. Last week we looked at transitions and this week sensory processing. Angela thought what better way to do this and to set up a big sensory play day. I didn't have to voice my concerns it was written all over my face, but my son has gone to some of these places with support workers so I might be over-reacting.

Inside, the Therapy Centre opens into a huge room with a kitchenette and tables on one side — the kind used for cooking independence tasks. Angela has divided it into a snack area and a wet play area. Beyond the tables is a large physiotherapy space. Off to the right are three smaller rooms, and at the far end, a set of double glass doors leads out to a lawn with water troughs for outdoor play.

I freeze, taking it all in. My heart rate spikes. My skin tingles. I can't tell if it's the sheer scope of the setup, the number of new people I'm supposed to remember, or just my social anxiety revving like an engine. My smile feels glued on — the kind you wear because you're supposed to, not because it fits. I can already feel the strain of holding myself together, of pretending this is fine when my nervous system is screaming that it isn't.

My eyes move before I consciously decide to look.

Area 1 — Movement Zone (Physio Room) Climbing wall. Ramp slide. Peanut balls. Mini trampoline. Gym mats. Lycra swings hanging like colourful cocoons. Double glass doors opening onto the lawn.

Area 2 — Builders Room Lego. Marble runs. Craft tables. Blocks stacked in neat piles.

Area 3 — Dry Sensory Room Rice tubs. Sand trays. Pasta scoops. Funnels and tools that make tiny engineers out of overwhelmed kids.

Area 4 — Quiet Room Weighted lap blankets. Sensory tents with fairy lights. Noise-reducing headphones. Soft music humming low.

Area 5 — Wet Sensory Area (Main Room) Slime tubs. Finger painting. Play-dough. Aprons already abandoned by children who don't believe in aprons.

Area 6 — Snack Tables (Kitchenette Side) A row of tables for kids to eat, reset, breathe.

Note for Angela – I know the intention was to let them choose and find what works for them but it's almost funny, how we're teaching sensory regulation by throwing every sensory input at them at once.

Ok maybe I should lose the sarcasm.

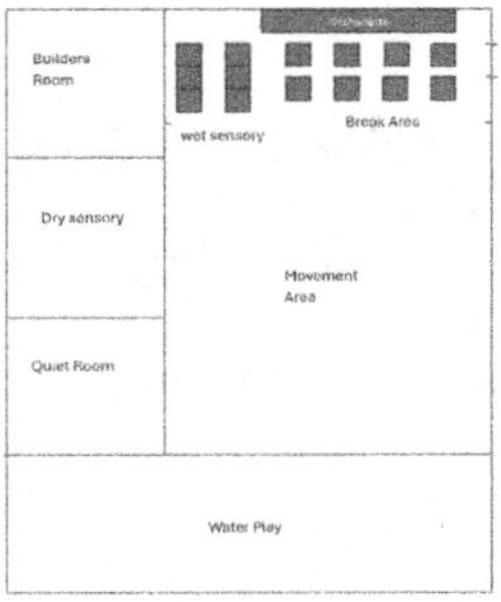

OT Centre

It's brilliant. It's thoughtful. To Archie this is heaven — he loves to explore — but for me it is chaos waiting to happen.

My brain starts cataloguing everything — exits, noise levels, potential triggers, safe corners — before I even realise I'm doing it. I start determining possible triggers for Archie and Violet. Then the noise level finally cuts through my dulled registration and I become overstimulated. I'm suddenly aware not only of the space but all the extra people I'll likely have to interact with today. Normally it's just ten adults at most, but today there are all the children to remember and navigate as well.

I was a high school teacher, so I'm used to being around children — but not like this and not with Archie. Archie struggles with young children; they're too unpredictable. And right now, I feel the same way.

I try to remember the kids and everyone else who would be here the way Angela told me, repeating them silently like flashcards:

Parents/ Guardians Children - descriptions

Janette and Samuel • Louise — Janette's sensory seeker

Priya and Norman • Joshua — Priya's tornado • Dale — Priya's careful child • Thinley — Priya's bossy princess

Martha and Edward • Allira — Martha's teen with attitude • Alex — Martha's boy

Tom • Arden — Tom's grandson

Sarah and Dave • Noah — Sarah's boy

Anna & Liam & Jace • Harry — Anna's boy

Kayla • Archie — my baby boy • Violet — my princess

This is way too much. Too many new things. I wonder whether, if I described today to someone else, if they'd feel as overwhelmed as I do with all this new information. I don't want to mix anyone up. This is the part people ignore when you have autistic children — adults can have anxiety and sensory processing challenges too. Sensory days can be fun for kids, but they can overload the adults just as easily.

Parents and guardians are already spreading out, settling into zones. I watch them move, watch their kids move, watch the room shift and swell around me. It's not the activities that make my chest tighten — I know how to navigate sensory spaces — it's the people. The conversations. The expectations. The pressure to be helpful, competent, friendly, all at once.

Archie presses into my side. Violet drifts toward the art tables like she's exhaling — she's always been my quiet observer, happiest when she can create something without anyone watching. I make a mental note to check in with her later, even though she looks fine. Quiet kids get overlooked too.

And I step forward, trying to look like I belong here.

My eyes sweep everything before I can stop them.

Louise bursts past us like a comet, braids already falling out. Janette whisper-yells, "Her questionnaire said full sensory seeker," clutching her notebook like a life raft. Louise spots the slime tub and becomes a force of nature. Joshua who was already there, joins, glitter shapes flying. I'm really hoping Archie doesn't want that area first.

Angela envelops me in a side hug and leads Thinley toward her brother Joshua and the finger paints.

Priya comforts Dale through his overwhelm and heads to the quiet room with him.

Allira collapses into a chair at the snack area, headphones on, teen attitude radiating like a force field. Martha helps her son Alex in the dry sensory room. Noah whizzes in and out of that room, drifting between stations, never settling. Sarah and her partner Dave trail behind. Tom sits with Arden and Violet at the craft table, already absorbed.

Archie clings to my side, overwhelmed by the people but excited by the place. His eyes dart from station to station, excitement and fear tangled together. I wish I could untangle it for him — give him a world that didn't overwhelm him before he even touched it.

My chest tightens. I'm trying to look calm, but my body is already bracing for impact knowing he will want to see everything. I take out his communication app and point to the visuals.

"Do you want the swing or the slime or the rice?" I ask.

He presses *swing*. We head into the quiet room and I help him into the Lycra — stretching, pulling, cocooning — a process that feels like origami with a child inside.

I stay near him, scanning the room again. Cataloguing, assessing, trying not to panic. There are windows in each of the smaller rooms so you can see out into the rest of the centre.

And then I see Jace. They're all here today — Jace, Anna, Liam, and Harry.

He's objectively hot. I'm not usually drawn to physiques — faces, smiles, actions are what get me — but his arms have me obsessed in a way I don't understand. Lean, sculpted, broad shoulders, steady hands. I look away before I embarrass myself, but the warmth rising in my chest doesn't fade. It's ridiculous how one person can make a room feel less hostile just by existing in it.

Anna and Liam head to the snack area for coffee while Jace takes Harry to the movement zone. He tries to bounce on a gym ball while stabilising Harry. The ball squeaks, shifts wrong, and Jace twirls like a dancer to save him. Somehow Harry moves too, and Jace ends up on the floor holding Harry above his face like a circus act. Anna laughs. I join her. Harry's socked feet hover near Jace's nose.

"That's what you get for helping my son avoid washing his socks," Anna calls.

The room erupts in laughter. I can't help but chuckle.

The chaos builds. Jace attempts a questionable gym ball trick, slides off in a slow, dignified arc, and winces — barely — the kind of wince you only catch if you've seen chronic pain before. Harry claps. Jace laughs, small and surprised.

Liam tries next, bounces once, slides off, lands on a mat looking betrayed, then laughs too. I feel myself loosen, just a little — like the room has shifted from threat to possibility.

Archie decides it's time to move to the builders' room.

Tom and Arden have also moved. Arden engineers marble runs with solemn precision. Tom watches with stunned pride. A little girl named Elsie traces textured tiles in the Lego pile. Archie's vocalisations scare her and she retreats to the quiet room. Angela notices and supports her without fuss.

Through the doorway, Noah becomes a blur — trampoline, swing, Lycra sock burrito. Priya wanders past, finger paints on her hands and a streak of blue on her cheek. Thinley bolts in and out of rooms, leaving fingerprints everywhere. Many kids get upset at her, and when she reaches Dale, a scream echoes in the distance.

I step out of the room, staying in the doorway so I can still see Archie.

It's beautiful chaos. It's also overstimulating. My brain is doing threat assessment, joy assessment, meltdown prediction, social masking — all at once. I stand there, surrounded by people, and still feel like I'm on the outside of a window looking in. I'm here to help, to support, to guide — but I'm not sure anyone actually sees me.

Then it happens.

Thinley rounds the room with Priya close behind, apologising to each person she terrorises even though the parents seem fine. As she passes the snack tables, Joshua flings glitter slime. It arcs through the air and lands squarely on Allira's face.

The room freezes. Of all the people to hit — not the angry teen.

Allira shrieks — outrage first, then delight — and launches after Thinley. Some kids join. Others are herded to safety. Chaos spikes.

Angela claps sharply. "Outside! Wet play outside only!"

The kids pour out the doors.

I turn to check Archie.

He is not fine.

He stands rigid, fists clenched, breath sharp. Glitter slime on his arm. Panic rising fast.

"Archie—"

He slams his forehead into the table.

The crack slices through me like lightning. Every instinct in my body screams to protect him, even from himself.

I sprint. He hits again. A parent steps forward.

"Please don't," I say, blocking them. "He can't handle new hands."

He screams — raw, tearing — and tries to slam again. I peel off my hoodie and slide it under his forehead just in time. He hits it hard.

This is why I protect his routines. This is why I avoid triggers. This is why I fight for accommodations. So, my beautiful boy doesn't hurt himself.

He swings at me. I don't react. Reacting makes it worse. Restraining him would escalate. I stay steady. Present. Quiet.

"It's okay, baby," I murmur. "You're safe. I'm right here."

He drops to his knees. I bring the hoodie to the floor in front of him. He collapses onto it, sobbing. I sit nearby, singing softly. His movements slow. His breathing steadies.

Relief hits me so hard it almost feels like grief. I hate that he hurts. I hate that this is our normal. And I hate that I'm already bracing for the next time.

Only then do I inch closer.

"Can I touch you?" I whisper.

He doesn't pull away. I place my hand on his back, apply deep pressure. He melts. Crawls into my lap. Anna notices and brings me things from the quiet room. I wrap him in a weighted blanket.

"You're safe," I whisper. "I've got you."

Sarah's partner Dave approaches. "You're... really good with him."

I shake my head. "Every kid's different. It's trial and error. What helps one day doesn't always help the next."

He nods and steps back.

Archie breathes against my collarbone. I kiss his hair. When he's ready, we move back toward the quiet area, but he spots the water play through the glass doors and wants to watch.

The kids — including Violet — shriek in the water play. Violet's laughter rings out, bright and unrestrained. Jace is on the tarp again, Harry on top of him, both laughing. Liam is soaked and smiling. Violet runs through the spray with Noah, her face lit up in a way I haven't seen in months.

Archie presses against me, calmer now, watching the water play with wide, curious eyes instead of fear. His breathing is steady against my shoulder.

A community. A moment of joy. And for the first time in a long time, I don't feel alone.

Every parent struggled today. Every child had a moment. It wasn't just me. Yes, Archie's meltdown was bigger, but here... here everyone understood.

Archie shifts, calmer now. I hold him close as we watch the madness.

About thirty minutes later, Angela has them tidying up outside and hands out towels. She pops her head in and asks if I can get the lunch area ready and bring out the fruit platters. The parents and children who remained inside — Dale, Priya, Martha, her husband, Alex, Sarah's partner, and Anna — join us at the snack area.

By the time everything is set up and the room tidied, the families gather for lunch and the session debrief. I feel exhausted but still hyper-alert — it never shuts off in social settings. My body is running on fumes, but my brain is still scanning, still listening, still bracing.

Angela talks about sensory processing and somehow gets everyone discussing how sensory needs change between people and even for the same person at different times of the day. She has a way of making complicated things feel simple, and I watch the parents soften as they realise they're not failing — they're learning.

When she mentions doing activities like these to meet sensory needs, Martha's husband looks horrified. I feel that familiar push to respond — the instinct to help, to ease someone's fear, even when I'm barely holding myself together.

"Angela means doing one activity from today in isolation, not everything at once," I say.

Relief washes over his face. I'm glad I'm not the only one overwhelmed. I'll have to talk to Angela about simplifying this day. Angela laughs, "Yes, exactly. It's important for children to learn to finish and clean up an activity before moving on. Routine and structure help the whole family."

I don't remember much more of the session. Even my hyper-alert state must falter after too much strain. I must have gone through the motions for the next twenty-four hours, because somehow we got home, had dinner, went to sleep, woke up, and made it to work and school.

Just another day surviving.

But as I replayed the chaos in my mind, one image kept returning — Jace laughing under a spray of water, Harry sprawled across him, the whole group erupting in joy. And beside them, Violet running through the spray with Noah, her face lit up in a way I hadn't seen in months. Archie pressed against me, calmer now, watching the water play with wide, curious eyes instead of fear.

It wasn't perfect. It wasn't easy. But it was the first time in a long time that both my kids found moments of happiness in the same place, at the same time, surrounded by people who understood them.

I didn't know what it meant. I didn't need to.

But it stayed with me — Jace's laugh, Violet's freedom, Archie's slow, steady breathing against my shoulder.

A snapshot of something I hadn't dared hope for: a community, a possibility, a life that didn't feel so isolating.

And maybe that was enough to carry me into tomorrow.

Chapter Eight

Truths I Didn't Want to See

Some days you ride the wave; other days the current pulls you under. But the way through is the same — don't fight the water. Learn its pull, and move with it.

Mickey's Blog Bits

Jace

Morning light spills through the blinds in thin, unforgiving stripes — too bright, too sharp, cutting across the room like it's trying to wake the dead. The air is already thick, that humid Perth heat that settles on the skin and makes everything feel heavier than it should.

The house is silent.

Not peaceful silent — hollow silent.

The kind that makes you too aware of your own breathing.

Sheets twisted around my legs. Stale sweat. A dull ache behind my eyes from another night of interrupted sleep and too many thoughts.

Two months in Perth and the days have started to blur — slow, soft, shapeless things. No plans. No goals. No hockey schedule keeping me moving. No purpose humming through my veins. Just sunlight, stillness, and the quiet throb of a life so far from what I dreamed. The only thing moving me is helping with Harry, a ridiculous crush on a brunette who ignores me and the unlikely friends I have made at the parent group

I roll over, trying to sink back into the nothingness, my phone vibrates on the bedside table.

Once. Twice. Then I recognised the ringtone — the one I haven't heard since I left Nashville.

Elliot. My rookie teammate. Left wing to my right. The kid who used to fly across the ice like he had rockets in his skates and something to prove.

I drag myself upright and answer.

"Yo, Jace," he says, voice rough like he's been shouting over rink noise all morning. "You still alive over there? Since Mel's not in the picture anymore, I figured one of the puck bunnies finally kidnapped you. If you didn't answer, I was about to alert search and rescue."

I manage a weak laugh. "Barely. And you know I stay away from puck bunnies. What's up?"

"Just finished drills. You missed the usual chaos — Coach Ivan's on a tear. Yelling at everyone like a drill sergeant on steroids."

I close my eyes, picturing Ivan's wild energy, the way he commands the rink like it's his kingdom. "Sounds about right."

"You remember that time you took that hit from me in practice? Thought I broke your ribs."

"Yeah, you forgot it was our job to move the puck not beat up the other players on the ice. Then the moment Ivan turned around you lined up the next puck like you were 100% focused on the warm-up."

He laughs, but it fades fast.

"It's not the same without you."

The line goes quiet — the kind of quiet that holds emotional heaviness.

"Yeah right," I say, trying to lighten it. "Without me showing you up, you'll get moved up to regular first string in no time."

He hesitates. I hear the tap tap tap of his skate blade against metal.

"Actually, I've been first string for a while and I was made captain yesterday," he says with a catch to his voice.

My chest tightens.

"I wasn't sure if I should ring," he adds, "but you were the first person — after my wife Nya — that I wanted to tell."

"I'm so happy for you, Elliot. You know I'll be watching your games. Cheering you on."

And I mean it.

But my stomach still drops.

"It's not fair, Jace. This should've still been you. I wouldn't be here without you. You taught me everything. You carried me through my rookie year."

I swallow hard. "Thanks, man. Means a lot."

"You know what you're gonna do next? More coaching? Colour Commentator? Something else? You'd be good at any of it."

"I... don't know who I am without being on the ice. And I'm no Ivan."

"You were one of the best captains I ever played with. I heard you were a great coach too. We were all shook up by what happened to Dalton, but that's exactly why we need coaches like you. Think about it."

The last thing I want to think about is Dalton – the accident, the aftermath, the helpless feeling that followed. It's why I've avoided hockey.

"I will," I say with reservation.

"If you ever need anything — tickets, merch, my signed jersey to impress a girl—"

I snort. "Yeah, yeah."

"Don't be a stranger, Jace."

"Let me know when you're settled in the new position. I'll call you then."

"Sounds good," before carefully adding, "Oh — call Mel. She's worried about you. And you said you'd stay friends, right?"

I take a deep breath, "Yeah we are, I'll call her today."

"Later, man."

"Later."

The call ends, and the room feels colder. Emptier.

I'm thrilled for him — genuinely — but I'm also... lost.

The only things giving me purpose right now are my family and a group of parents who couldn't be more different from anyone I've known before.

I pull up Mel's contact and I decide to call her office.

Better get this done.

It rings twice.

"Public Relations Department, Predators Hockey, Melanie Jansen speaking."

"Hey Mel. It's Jace."

A sharp inhale. "Where the hell have you been? I've been trying to reach you for weeks. I thought we were still friends."

"I thought giving you space might help."

"Space?" Her voice cracks like a whip. "I didn't want to break up, remember? I still love you, Jace. I would've come to Australia with you."

Her words hit hard — but the truth hits harder.

"Mel... you had just been promoted. Your career was taking off. I didn't want to drag you down. Plus, we had been separated for ten months before I left."

"Yes, but I understood you needed a break and wanted to deal with the PTSD relapse yourself. We were still close friends. I could've sorted things out and taken vacation days," she fires back.

"Mel, I'm fighting a lot of inner battles right now. It would've ruined your vacation."

"You think you're the only one fighting battles? You think I don't have my own chaos? But I'm here. I'm still here. I'm not letting you fade away."

Her voice softens. "You're not alone, Jace. Not while I'm around."

The line goes quiet. Too quiet.

"Mel... I need to be brutally honest."

I hear her breath hitch.

"You're amazing. You were always my most loyal friend. My cheerleader. My partner in everything off the ice. And I spent three years trying to give you back everything you gave me. I wanted to love you."

A soft, broken sob slips through the speaker.

"I was raised to treat women right," I say quietly. "To be loyal. To show up. And I tried. I really did."

Her sobs get louder.

"I love the idea of love, Mel. But if it had been you who lost everything... I wouldn't have given up hockey for you. And that's not love. Not the kind you deserve."

Silence. Then a whisper: "Jace... I need to go. I'll... I'll call—"

"I'm sorry, Mel. I know you'll find someone better."

A broken sounding, "Bye" comes through just as the call ends.

I never wanted to break her.

I didn't tell her everything. I couldn't. I didn't want her to sacrifice and say it didn't matter to her when I knew it did.

A memory flickers — one I've buried so deep it shouldn't still hurt.

The doctor's office. Cold room. Colder words.

"Your pelvic ring injury caused more internal damage than we initially realised."

I remember nodding like it was nothing. Like he'd told me I'd sprained a wrist.

Then the rest of it hit.

"Your fertility may be affected. Significantly."

I sat there in silence, staring at the floor tiles, counting them so I wouldn't fall apart. I was twenty-seven. My career was gone. My body was broken. And now this.

I didn't tell Mel. Couldn't.

She always talked about having a family someday — the house, the kids, the life she'd dreamed of since she was little.

She deserved the family she constantly talked about. Not a man who couldn't promise any of it.

I had watched the other players' relationships, and I knew I was being selfish. I loved her as a friend — but not as a man who has found someone he couldn't bear to lose.

She deserved someone who adored her. Someone who could give her a future. A life that wasn't built on compromises and medical maybes.

Not me.

And it's not just that. I haven't been able to tell anyone.

You go through the stages of grief — denial first, always denial — and somehow it feels shameful. Like I'm not enough of a man. Like something in me failed.

I never really thought about kids. Not beyond wanting to give Mel what she wanted. That was the whole point back then — be what she needed, tick the boxes, keep the peace.

But now, helping with Harry... I can see the pros and cons. I can picture what it might look like. A kid who laughs like that. A kid who trusts me like that.

But it's not the possibility of not having a child that gets under my skin. It's the feeling of being less than. Like I've lost something I didn't even know was important until it was gone. And I'm not a hundred percent sure what that is exactly.

Chapter Nine

Masking, Mental Health, and the Cost of Holding It All Together

Masking is survival — choosing the version of yourself least likely to be misunderstood or rejected. But every time you hold it together, you lose a little of the self you're hiding. Your quirky spark. Your creative parts. The parts that were never meant to be trimmed down to fit. The cost of safety is always yourself.

Mickey's Blog Bits

Kayla

Another parent session, this was week number ten. As I looked around the table at our group, I could see the weight of the previous week sitting on everyone's shoulders. The energy in the room was low. Even the coffee wasn't helping.

Angela started the group with her usual sunny exuberance. "Okay everyone. Let's review the topics we've covered over the last nine weeks."

Sarah shot her hand up like an over-eager student before remembering we could just speak. "Diagnosis and Labels, Autistic traits, developing social skills and behaviour as communication."

"Communication Differences, repetitive and restrictive behaviours, Advocacy" Janette added.

"Sensory processing and why it drives everything," offered Priya, clearly still thinking about how important that session had been for her.

“Self-care,” grinned Anna, looking directly at me.

“Excellent,” Angela said. “The last nine weeks have been a crash course in understanding our kids and supporting the main features associated with autism and ADHD. Now we’re moving into the things connected to these diagnoses that aren’t as obvious.”

She paused, letting the shift settle.

“As you’ll notice, this is the deeper side of disability. The part no one warns you about. The part that doesn’t just shape our kids — it shapes us. We’re talking about mental health, functioning, and identity.”

I knew I had to add something. As amazing as Angela was, she hadn’t lived much of this herself. “When we start talking about mental functioning and mental health, there will be some confronting stories and discussions. Please feel free to excuse yourself and grab a cuppa if you need a breather. And if any of this hits deeper and you feel you need extra support, Angela has details about services you can access.”

Angela gave me a grateful smile. I whispered, “Don’t forget the content warnings.”

She nodded and turned back to the group.

“Let’s read today’s story from Mickey. It covers masking, depression, and a form of self-criticism known as Rejection Sensitivity Dysphoria.”

Flashback — Mickey Age 13

“They’re not coming.”

I remember saying it out loud into my empty bedroom, my voice cracking like something inside me had snapped. The tension shot through my nerves so fast it felt electric. My mind raced with the same old voices that had been rehearsing their lines for years:

No one likes you. You're weird. You're not special. You will always be alone. This is why you never get invited to things, Mickey.

The thoughts blurred into a storm of self-loathing, disappointment, frustration, sadness, and anger. I paced the room in heavy, stomping steps, each one shaking loose more emotion than my body knew how to hold.

Dad tried to intervene — I don't remember what he said — because by then I was already crying, bellowing, overwhelmed. And then the shame hit. It always did. That hot, choking shame that told me I was "overreacting," even though another part of me was screaming:

I have reason to feel this way. I have reason to hurt. I have reason to cry.

And then — the sound of a car horn outside.

My friend had arrived. A car full of girls ready to go to the ice rink. Girls who were laughing, excited, normal. Girls who didn't know that five minutes earlier I'd been falling apart.

I had seconds.

Seconds to breathe. Seconds to shove everything down. Seconds to slip on the mask I'd been perfecting since I was old enough to talk.

I smoothed out my burgundy shirt — plain, loose, safe — over my denim jeans. I didn't know it then, but this was the a clear example of my rules. My armour. The quiet dictatorship I enforced on myself with ruthless precision:

- Wear plain clothing. One colour. No pattern. Never anything bold.
- Never stand out.
- Position yourself in blind spots — corners, edges, shadows.
- Watch and listen, but don't talk unless you've rehearsed the script.
- If the conversation goes off script, leave.
- Never talk to boys when girls are around. Girls get territorial.
- Above all else: do not draw attention to yourself.

I walked out the door smiling like nothing had happened but my nervous system was still on fire.

Kayla

The room was silent when Angela finished reading.

Not the uncomfortable kind — the heavy kind. The kind where everyone was sitting with their own memories, their own children, their own versions of Mickey's thirteen-year-old panic.

Angela let out a whoosh of breath before she spoke.

"This," she said softly, "is what masking and Rejection Sensitivity Disorder or RSD can look like from the inside. Not dramatic. Not attention-seeking. Just survival."

Priya exhaled first. "I see this in Dale every day. The rigidity. The panic when plans change. The way he shuts down if he thinks someone is disappointed in him."

Janette nodded. "For Louise, it's the rules. Her rules. If anything shifts even a little, she spirals. I used to think it was stubbornness. Now I realise it's fear."

Sarah rubbed her forehead. "Noah apologises before he even knows what he's apologising for. If someone sighs, he thinks it's about him. If someone laughs, he thinks they're laughing at him. It's exhausting for him. And for us."

I looked down at my hands. "Violet masks so hard at school that she collapses the second she gets home. I used to worry she was depressed, but now I know it's burnout. Burnout from masking. Burnout from fear created by wanting to belong when you feel different. It's the overwhelm when constructive critique feels like a damning report card on your latest failure. When one look is misconstrued as disappointment. When the smallest thing that goes wrong determines your whole day — or makes it feel like your world is imploding."

I scanned the faces around the room, feeling an uncomfortable vulnerability settle in my chest. My internal supervisor Overthinker Owen dragged Overshare Olivia into a chokehold, his eyes wide as he signalled to Factoid Frank to salvage the situation.

“There are great resources by ADHD Alien,” I added quickly. “She has incredible comics on what RSD looks like and how to support someone experiencing it.”

Thank you, Factoid Frank.

I breathed deeply, grateful when Angela took over.

“Masking is a full-time job,” she said gently. “And our kids start doing it long before they have the words for it. They hide their overwhelm, their confusion, their sensory pain, their fear of rejection. And when they finally get home — to the place and people that make them feel safest — everything spills out.”

Murmurs of agreement circled the table.

“And RSD,” she continued, “isn't just sensitivity. It's a nervous system response. A threat response. A belief that rejection is coming — even when it isn't.”

I swallowed, eager to escape the intensity swirling in my chest.

Priya leaned forward. “I'll look up ADHD Alien, but in the meantime... what do we do? How do we help them?”

Angela smiled — not her sunshine smile, but the soft, steady one she saved for the hard topics.

“We teach them what's in the rest of Mickey's blog — the things she learned as an adult.

We teach them to love themselves the way they are. We teach them that difference is okay — and worth celebrating. We teach them confidence, and how to stop people-pleasing for acceptance. We teach them that a small setback is not a for the rest of their day or life. We teach them to pause. To check the facts. To breathe. To separate fear from reality. To trust us enough to bring the meltdown to us instead of hiding it.”

She looked around the table, meeting each of our eyes.

“And we do the same for ourselves. Because many of us grew up masking too. Many of us survived the same way Mickey did — by shrinking, smoothing, disappearing.”

A quiet hum of recognition moved through the room and at that moment I had come to realise how much Angela had listened and learnt.

Jace

At first, these conversations about masking and RSD were just fascinating insights into struggles other people dealt with. I'd always been popular in school. Hockey captain. Always felt like I belonged. I never felt a need to mask. The closest I ever came to catastrophising was the few times I got caught up in game superstitions.

Then Kayla spoke about Violet.

And suddenly I felt it — the swirl of thoughts, the misunderstandings, the way one small thing could eat at your confidence. I felt something I couldn't name. A desire to protect, maybe. But also, a quiet recognition that when the glamour and popularity of hockey began to fade... maybe I felt this too.

Especially when Angela talked about the strategies.

"Teach them that a small setback is not a prophecy for the rest of their day or life."

Wasn't I doing exactly that? Okay, hockey-wise it was huge. But life-wise?

I know I'm not experiencing what these kids do every day, when they have to mask who they are and feel less than because of it, but I could see the value of the strategies for everyone.

I drifted into my thoughts until Anna nudged me.

Angela's voice pulled me back. "Over the next few weeks, we're going to talk about the deeper layers: executive functioning, polyvagal states, depression, suicidal ideation, trauma. Not because your children are experiencing this or because you're failing — but because statistics show a high prevalence of these experiences in autistic and ADHD people."

My shoulders tightened.

This was a whole new world for me. But if I was honest... I knew I'd been experiencing bouts of depression. Maybe this wasn't just about Harry anymore.

Angela clapped her hands lightly. "Alright. Before we wrap up — tell me one thing you've noticed in your child this week that makes more sense after hearing Mickey's story."

Parents shared one by one:

- "The way he freezes when someone raises their voice."
- "Her panic when her friend didn't reply immediately."
- "The meltdown after school that wasn't about the shoes at all."
- "The way he copies everyone else to fit in."
- "The rules she invents to feel safe."

When it was my turn, I shrugged. "I haven't noticed anything in Harry, but he is very obsessed with his blue cup."

Anna laughed. "I've noticed rigidity like Jace said, but..."

Kayla stepped in gently. "Harry is only five. A lot of behaviours we associate with masking and sensitivity are hard to distinguish at this age. All children copy. All children feel big emotions without the ability to regulate them."

I looked at Anna, relieved we weren't just clueless.

Angela nodded. "Exactly. The aim of these sessions is to help you with what you *are* noticing — not to make you see things that aren't there or doubt your own abilities."

The session ended, but the weight of it stayed with me — not heavy, just real.

Chapter Ten

Splish Splash and the Banana Show

Different needs. Different tools. Build the life that fits the people you love, instead of forcing them to bend to a world that wasn't built with them in mind.

Mickey's Blog Bits

Jace

It's been three days since that conversation with Mel and I still feel like I got blindsided on open ice. I keep replaying it — the way my voice went cold, the way she went quiet. I didn't mean to hit her that hard. I just... couldn't keep pretending that there was a possibility that we could get back together. Couldn't drag someone into the storm I'm skating through.

And the guilt won't let up.

I don't know why I'm on edge today. Maybe because the last few days have been one long reminder that my life is off its game — career gone, confidence shot, barely keeping things steady for Harry. I shouldn't be thinking about anything else. Anyone else.

But then Anna hands me Harry's bag and then casually says

"Oh — I forgot. I organised for Harry to do some baking with Kayla today. Can you take him?" Just like that, she drops it on me, like it's nothing.

Kayla.

My brain just... stalls. Like a goalie freezing the puck.

There's this flicker in my chest — the first spark of anything good in months — and right behind it, nerves. The kind I haven't felt since I was a rookie walking into a locker room full of guys who'd already earned their place. The kind that makes you suddenly aware your tough-guy armour has a few cracks in it.

I shut it down fast because Anna is a heat-seeking missile when it comes to me showing even the slightest interest in a woman. Before Mel, she tried to set me up with anyone who so much as made eye contact. I'm not giving her a reason to start that again. Not when I don't even know what the hell is happening in my own head.

I see Kayla every group session. Sometimes when she grabs coffee with Anna. She's... something else. Beautiful, yeah, but that's not the thing that draws me to . It's the way she talks. The way she sees people. The way she calmed Harry in the store like she'd been doing it her whole life — steady, patient, zero judgement.

Every group session, she says something that knocks me sideways. Sarah knows the textbook stuff, but Kayla talks like she's lived it. Like she's been in the trenches with kids like Harry and caregivers like me. When the topic was behaviour, Sarah explained the ABCs. Kayla explained what it *looks* like at home. What it *feels* like when you're the parent trying not to fall apart.

Her voice is always calm. Kind. Never making anyone feel stupid.

And every time she talks, something in me loosens.

Which is exactly why I can't be feeling this pull toward her. Not now. Not when I'm barely holding my own life together. Not when I just hurt someone who didn't deserve it. But here I am — standing at Kayla's front door, Harry bouncing beside me, and my chest doing that tight, hopeful thing I don't trust anymore. I'm not ready for this. I'm not ready for *her*.

But I'm already here. Already knocking. Already wondering why the thought of seeing her hits me harder than it should.

And that scares me more than I want to admit.

I turn to the window near the door; Archie is staring at us through the glass. He's wearing only briefs... or maybe a nappy. Hard to tell. He's just standing there, expression blank, like we're the entertainment.

Harry doesn't seem fazed at all. Of course he doesn't.

Now I can hear noises — long, low, vibrating sounds, almost like throat singing. Not words. Not humming. Just the kind of prolonged vocalisation — a sound that fills the space without meaning to.

I knock again.

"Coming!"

The door flies open and, in a blink-and-you'll-miss-it moment, Kayla moves from the doorway into the next room, like she teleported.

"Come in. I am running behind this morning. I need to shower Archie and then we will start the baking. The remote is there — put on the banana show for Harry and he will be fine for a moment."

Before I can even nod, she asks Google to Play the song Splish Splash.

The music fills the room and Kayla starts singing along.

The boy from the window — Archie — immediately runs to her. Kayla looks down at him and says warmly, "Shower."

He echoes back, "Shower," like a confirmation — echolalia they called it in group I think. Then he takes her hand.

They disappear down the hallway, and she keeps singing, louder now, like she's performing for a stadium.

She has a great voice. I'd be confident singing too if I sounded like that.

I'm left standing there, stunned, trying to take it all in — the chaos, the singing, the near-naked Archie, the fact that Kayla moves like she's powered by caffeine and adrenaline.

Then I hear Harry behind me.

"Na-na so."

I turn. He's pointing at the TV.

I find the remote, hit play, and Harry immediately sits on the floor like he's entered a trance.

I sit down on the couch, watching Harry engrossed in the TV show, and I can't help but smile.

This little man has become everything to me in the last month. I never really thought about being a father and I'm still definitely not wanting all-nighters with babies, but I can't deny the fulfilment of watching him grow and being a part of it. My mind goes back to Kayla. She can sing — properly sing — and from our previous encounters I thought she was a little uptight, but now... maybe not so much.

Fifteen minutes later, Kayla returned, half-soaked, hair sticking to her cheek, with a fully dressed Archie trotting along behind her.

“Sorry about that,” she said, not sounding sorry at all — more like resigned. “Things didn’t go according to plan this morning.”

She didn’t wait for me to speak. Barely looked at me, actually.

Instead, she crouched down to Harry’s level.

“Harry,” she said warmly, “should we make cookies or cupcakes?”

Harry sat there, contemplating the decision like it was a matter of national importance.

Shocked, I blurted out, “You called it cookies!”

She laughed — a real laugh, bright and unguarded. “Too much Sesame Street. Before I had Archie, I called them biscuits.”

She stood and clapped her hands lightly. “Archie, come sit up at the table. You too, Harry. Okay — what are we making? Cookies or cupcakes?”

“Cupcake,” Archie echoed immediately.

“CUH CAY!” Harry yelled, as if announcing the winner of a game show.

“Cupcakes it is,” Kayla said, handing each of us an apron. “Trust me — you’ll need this.”

She gathered ingredients from the pantry, then showed the boys a recipe sheet with pictures of cupcakes.

She becomes a whirlwind of motion, setting everything set up like she is running on instinct. Then she stops abruptly and scans the room. Her gaze lands on me. I'm not sure what expression I'm wearing – amazement, maybe - but she winces and says, "Sorry, I can be very task orientated." Then she smiles and motions to the ingredients, “Can you help me measure all of this into bowls? It’ll make it easier for them to join in.”

I came around to her side of the bench and looked at the ingredients while she collected bowls and measuring cups. Flour was first on the list, so I grabbed the bag. She handed me the measuring cup, and I poured two cups of flour into the bowl and pushed it to the side in front of me.

I was about to move on to the butter, as Kayla was already pouring milk — when a flour bomb detonated in my direction.

It was like time froze.

A white cloud hung in the air. I stood there, covered. Kayla froze mid-pour. Harry stared, wide-eyed. And Archie... Archie was rocking back and forth, hands flapping joyfully, eyes bright.

Then Kayla burst out laughing.

I stayed stock-still for a few seconds, processing the explosion, before I started laughing too. Harry and Archie were grinning like they'd witnessed the best magic trick ever.

Kayla was laughing so hard she doubled over, struggling to catch her breath. When she finally straightened, she wiped her eyes and said, "I should have warned you not to put anything in front of Archie."

I looked over at him. He was pushing his hands — then his arms — through the flour, rubbing it up to his shoulders like it was the world's best lotion.

"He's a sensory seeker," Kayla explained. "When he was eighteen months old, I took him to a baby group. They put butcher's paper on the floor and dropped blobs of paint around the babies. All the other babies moved away. Archie dove straight into the paint — belly-sliding through it, spreading it everywhere. He had the best time while all the other babies just stared at him."

"What did you do?" I asked.

"At first I was shocked, I tried to pull him off the paint. But the play leader told me to let him explore. And he was so happy... so I let him go." She pointed to a framed photo on the wall — a tiny Archie, covered head-to-toe in paint, grinning like he'd discovered joy itself. "I realised then he was different. And that letting him be who he is was more important than anything else."

She looked back at the flour-covered bench and smirked. "We'll leave this mess for now and keep going. But don't put any liquids near the boys." she sassed me.

I saluted her. "Noted."

We continued measuring ingredients — carefully this time — and helped the boys mix everything together and spoon the batter into cupcake trays. Kayla suggested the boys could watch TV or go on the swings while the cupcakes baked.

Archie and Harry bolted outside toward the swings like they'd been launched.

Kayla and I stood in the sudden quiet, both dusted in flour and pretending not to notice how close we were standing.

We cleaned the bench, set out bowls of icing and sprinkles, and awkwardly made small talk — the kind where you're both trying not to stare at each other too long. I needed to find a way to break the tension before I did something stupid.

"You're so good at this," I blurted. She looked at me confused, "Cupcakes?"

"No parenting," I corrected. She laughed, as she started busying herself with the dishes. "I'd learned the hard way that reacting never worked. Reacting meant meltdowns and overwhelm for both of us. Reacting meant I was always two steps behind. So I learnt to be proactive, look for tools that suited us, like musical cues to routines. I'm just like every other parent doing my best. I have my moments where I struggle. Preparing has become everything."

She talked about it nonchalantly, like it was nothing out of the ordinary. As ordinary as the dishes she was currently washing while avoiding looking at me

"First I learned to:

- keep the flour on the top shelf, far from curious hands
- use songs instead of repeated instructions
- set up the environment before Archie enters it
- remove triggers before they became problems
- build routines that felt safe, predictable, and kind

and second, I learned to

- manage my own overwhelm as much as possible.

It isn't magic. Just transformed support"

I was amazed by her, the lilt of her voice drawing me in, it was beyond my control. I had to get a hold of myself. I forced myself to think of something other than the way her dark brown curls bounced against her shoulders as she worked. I thought about her words instead. Replaying them for a long time, eventually shaking my head, even with preparation I could not be this good with the kids.

When the cupcakes were done and cooled, Kayla tapped the door with a wooden spoon and started singing softly: " *Five more minutes, five more minutes,* when the alarm goes its sprinkle time. "

That's when the **real** chaos began.

Not delicate cupcake decorating

Sprinkles everywhere. Icing on faces. Archie trying to eat the decorations straight from the bowl. Harry insisting the banana toy needed its own cupcake.

At first we were laughing and then Archie's sensory threshold tipped — too much noise, too much colour, too much everything — and he started to unravel.

Before I could even panic, Kayla moved.

Lights dimmed. Blanket over Archie's shoulders. Deep pressure hug. Fidget toy in his hand. Soft humming.

He melted into her like she was the only anchor he had.

I watched her — calm, steady, instinctive — and something in my chest shifted.

This woman wasn't uptight. She wasn't cold. She wasn't distant.

She faced the world in a completely different way to me.

Chapter Eleven

Coffee and Lines Crossed

Self-pity used to be my default setting — a righteous anger I wore like armour. But I broke up with that enabler. I don't need sympathy to survive. I don't need someone else to make me happy. I outgrew that a long time ago.

Mickey's Blog Bits

Kayla

Just as Archie was settling, I heard a knock on the door. I knew that knock. I knew exactly who it was. And I wasn't surprised.

"Come in, Anna," I called.

From the corner of my eye, I saw Jace spin around in confusion.

"Anna? I thought I was bringing Harry home at five," he said.

"I finished work early and thought I'd relieve you. Plus, I came to see Kayla," she added, wearing that innocent look she absolutely practiced in the mirror.

"Alright, I'll head home. I might make it before the Nashville Predators game starts. My friend should be captaining the game today. See you, Kayla," he said, waiting for me to acknowledge him.

"Bye," I called, already walking toward the kitchen. "Coffee, Anna?"

"You know it," she replied. Then, softer, to Jace, "Thanks for today."

I heard the door open and close as I started making the coffee.

Soft footsteps approached behind me.

"Looks like everyone had a lot of fun today," Anna said with a grin.

"Don't play coy, Anna. I know what you're trying to do."

Her tone turned sugary sweet — the kind that could rot teeth. "What am I trying to do?"

"Don't think I can't see past your angelic farce. You're trying to set me up with Jace."

"Not set up," she corrected, smirking. "Just... push you together and see if anything blooms."

"Don't you think you should fix your own relationship first?" I snapped before I could stop myself.

Her face fell.

Instant regret hit me like a punch to the stomach.

"Crap. Sorry, Anna. I wasn't trying to stab you where it hurts. I just want you to stop. You know how I feel about relationships. You and Liam are made for each other — you'll work it out. Just keep talking. But please don't interfere in my life. I have my reasons"

Anna lowered her head slightly. "Sorry. I'm just fond of you, and I love Jace, and I thought... how perfect would it be if something happened between you two."

I handed her the freshly made coffee. "I promise I'll work on getting to know him as a friend. Then we can still have game nights or whatever you're planning in that head of yours."

She chuckled — the genuine one, the one that meant we were okay.

I didn't have a lot of friends. At one time, that bothered me. Now... I'd found my own happiness. I didn't rely on other people to give it to me. Long weeks or months without seeing friends didn't scare me anymore. I knew I could call the few I had if I needed them, and they could call me.

I had my family. My children. My sisters. My dad.

That was enough.

Meeting Anna — becoming close to her — had been exactly what I needed as Archie grew more social. I knew she'd be a friend for life. But I also knew there would come a time when life got busy and we'd see each other less. And that was okay.

We spent the next hour chatting while entertaining the kids. Archie and Harry were in the middle of a tickle standoff when Anna asked the one question I was rarely asked.

"Kayla... where is Archie and Violet's father? Don't you find it tough to go it alone?"

I didn't feel anything. Not sadness. Not loss. Just that familiar shift inside me — the one that made me watch her face for judgement before it had a chance to land.

"You know I have strong faith," I said. She nodded, though her expression tightened with something like concern.

"Twelve years ago, I was a lot more black-and-white about it than I am now," I added, trying to soften the air between us. "My specialist told me that if I wanted children, I needed to have them soon. And I have always been... terrible at relationships." I gave a small laugh, because that's what people expect when you admit something like that. "One day I'll tell you the stories. They're ridiculous."

Her eyes flickered — pity, sympathy, something I didn't want.

I hated pity. I am no victim. Pity was useless.

"So," I continued, keeping my voice steady, "I made a decision a lot of people in my old circles judged me for. I chose IVF with a donor."

Her eyes widened. There was a pause — a long one — as she waited for me to break, or cry, or confess something heavy.

I felt none of that.

She finally exhaled and asked, "Do you... know the donor's identity?"

There it was — curiosity, not judgement. Good. That mattered more than anything else.

"No," I said. "By law, I only got a list of characteristics. The kids can access the identity when they turn eighteen."

Her shoulders relaxed. The tension left her face. And just like that, the moment passed.

To her, it was a revelation. To me, it was nothing more than a fact — the safest part of my story.

She nodded, chewing her lip. "I couldn't imagine choosing to do this alone. I really struggle even when Liam and Jace are there to help. It would be easier if I went home and I know Liam agreed to the assessment for Harry... but I still don't feel ready to go back."

I reached over and hugged her. "Only you can decide when you've had enough space to communicate your needs and whether you see enough action in return. You can always come to me if you need anything. Thanks for being here for me too, Anna."

We talked for another hour, watching the boys play next to each other with brief, gentle interactions. To most people, it would look like nothing. But for my boy, this was huge.

I told myself — again — that my children were all I needed right now. They needed me to give them everything. One day, I'd travel again, follow my passions, learn new hobbies. But right now, they were my everything.

I knew that thinking was dangerous. After years of burnout, I was only just starting to allow myself some self-care.

And somewhere in the back of my mind — a place I refused to look directly at — I could still feel the faint echo of Jace's presence in my home.

I pushed it away. Hard.

There were lines I didn't cross. Not then. Not yet.

Chapter Twelve

Thunderstruck Mornings

> People love tidy definitions, as if autism is one set of traits, one way of functioning, one predictable pattern. Parents of multiple autistic kids know better. Autism is a spectrum that moves. It changes shape from child to child, and from morning to morning in the same child. It's a sand sculpture — constantly reshaped by the smallest change in wind or tide.
>
> Mickey's Blog Bits

Kayla

I jerk awake to AC/DC's *Thunderstruck* blasting through the house — not the soft buildup of the song I'm supposed to wake up to, but the full Bon Scott screech that hits like a defibrillator to the soul.

So much for easing into the morning. I must have been tired to have slept through so much of the song.

Six months ago, I learned this trick about using music for transitions. It's helped me stay calm. There are only so many times you can say each part of the routine before you start getting frustrated. This way, the song is the reminder, and I can focus on everything else.

I groan, roll out of bed, and blink through the fog of another too-late night. I've never been a morning person, and motherhood didn't fix that. If anything, it made it worse — clinging to scraps of time at night, then paying for it at dawn.

I shuffle down the hall and push open Archie's door.

"Please no mess, please no mess..." I whisper.

Relief floods me.

No bowel accidents. No food smeared on the walls. Sheets dry. A miracle.

Archie looks up from his bed, hair wild, eyes bright.

"Hungry?" I ask.

"Pies," he says immediately — soft voice, firm tone.

"How about toast? Crunchy Nut?"

"Pies."

"Pancakes?"

"Pies."

I sigh. Safe foods it is.

Pie crusts, no meat. Dry noodles. Plain white bread. Macaroni cheese with barely enough cheese to qualify.

I head to the kitchen and put four Pattie's party pies in the air fryer — no other brand will do. The hum of it fills the quiet.

Violet appears in the doorway, already dressed, hair brushed, bag packed. She looks like a tiny adult in an oversized school uniform.

"You look ready for school," I say. "Homework done?"

She nods, rubbing her eyes. She's not a morning person either, but she's always up early on school days. She hates being rushed. And yet I don't think I've ever known a morning where I wasn't.

"Do you want breakfast?" I ask.

She shrugs. "Maybe toast."

I put bread in the toaster with one hand while pulling out a plate with the other and checking the air fryer. Archie wanders in, flapping softly, pacing back and forth between the fridge and the pantry over and over. Violet sits at the table, quietly organising her pencil case for the third time.

Two kids. Two completely different people with different needs. Just one me.

Archie needs help with every step of the morning routine — dressing, toileting, eating, brushing teeth, getting to the Ed support school bus.

Violet needs calm, predictability, and someone to notice her even when she doesn't ask.

I try to split myself down the middle. Most days, it feels like I'm failing.

"Toast's ready," I say, sliding a plate to Violet.

"Thanks, Mum."

I hear a beep; the pies are done. I complete the well-practised ritual: cut the top off, scrape the meat from the lid, scoop the filling out of the base, leaving only the empty crust, his safe food. Archie eats the tops first, methodical, focused.

I glance at the clock. The bus will be here in twenty minutes. Violet's gifted program drop-off after that. Her therapy pickup later. My dentist appointment... yeah, that's not happening.

I'll reschedule. Again.

Archie finishes eating and I guide him through dressing — shirt over his head, socks that never quite cooperate, shoes that are often on the wrong feet. Violet quietly packs her lunch, watching us with that mix of patience and resignation that breaks my heart.

I want to be more present for her. I want to split myself evenly. But mornings are triage, and Archie's needs shout louder.

The bus pulls up. I walk Archie out, hand his bag over, and wave once he's seated.

When I come back inside, Violet is standing by the door with her bag.

"Ready?" she asks.

"Yeah," I say, going to grab my keys.

Violet gives me that look — the one that says she already knows I've misplaced them. I pull out my phone and connect to the Air Tag. Thank goodness for technology. I follow the beeping and locate my keys.

"Let's go."

As we head out, my phone buzzes — a reminder for the parent group.

I swipe it away.

I can't go today. Violet needs to be picked up early for therapy. And honestly... I'm too tired to support Angela today.

I'm not sure when it changed, but some weeks I feel like I don't want to just be the person sharing experiences who will leave this group and move to the next. I really like these people. I connect with them. I've been on this journey a long time now, and people often look to me as a source of insight and experience.

They get their answers and they move on — but I don't want that here.

Sometimes I'm relieved when all they do is talk about Mickey and the blog, though they've honestly become a bit obsessive. They're reading the full posts outside the group and commenting on them. I should steer them to other autistic voices, but I haven't.

No — that would make me the expert again. And I want to just be one of them. Because here, I get to be me — terrified, vulnerable me. Not openly. Not fully. Not yet. But enough that I don't have to script every sentence to help someone else on their journey.

I feel guilty thinking that. I remember what it was like to be new to all this. I want to help. But...

Some days, wanting more feels possible. And other days — like today — survival is enough.

Chapter Thirteen

The Self-Care Sacrifice

There are days we convince ourselves we're doing fine. That if we just keep putting one foot in front of the other, we'll eventually land somewhere better. Tomorrow we'll fix it. Tomorrow we'll rest. Tomorrow we'll feel like ourselves again. But sometimes we don't need a better tomorrow. Sometimes we need a drastic intervention today — even if we're the last ones to realise it.

Mickey's Blog Bits

Jace

Liam, Anna, Harry and I walk into the parent group and the first thing I notice is the empty chair.

Kayla's chair.

I didn't realise how much I'd come to rely on her presence until I saw that space — calm, steady, quietly holding everyone together without even trying.

Angela noticed me staring.

She clapped her hands once, gently. "Alright everyone. Change of plans. Kayla isn't able to be here today. She's so busy she cancelled her own dentist appointment. Which made me think... maybe we need to revisit self-care."

A few parents groaned.

Priya muttered, "I don't even have time to pee alone."

Angela smiled. “Exactly.”

Before she could continue, Sarah’s hand shot up like she was about to burst. “Oh! Mickey has a whole series on this — spoons, buckets, the self-care wheel— “

Priya smiled at her indulgently, shaking her head. “You’ve read all of them.”

“Twice,” Sarah said proudly.

Martha added, “Her posts make you feel less alone. I wish I had them five years ago.”

The group nodded.

They weren’t just fans. They were devoted — like the most diehard hockey fans or blog heads, living and breathing every moment on the ice or, in this case, the blog.

I didn’t get it yet. But I would.

Angela held up a laminated circle. “The self-care wheel. It has six separate areas of self-care. Most of us only think of one or two. But autistic people — and their parents — often sacrifice entire categories just to get through the day.”

Tom snorted. “I’m lucky if I hit one.”

“Same,” Priya said. “My self-care is drinking my coffee before it goes cold.”

“That counts,” Angela said. “Small things matter.”

Martha leaned forward. “I agree with Mickey’s statement — self-care isn’t bubble baths. It’s functioning maintenance. Like charging a phone. You can’t run on 1% forever.”

Angela nodded. “Today we’re doing something different. Pair up. Go through the wheel. Talk about what you need, what you actually get, and what stops you.”

The room split. Sarah with Priya. Janette with Martha. Liam with Anna. I ended up with Tom.

He was easy to talk to — blunt, steady — but even then, I couldn’t be honest or real.

We went through the wheel. Physical. Emotional. Cognitive. Sensory. Social. Spiritual.

Every category felt like a test I was failing.

Tom admitted he barely slept. I heard Priya crying quietly in the corner. Saw Janette staring at her worksheet like it was written in another language.

And me?

I kept thinking about Harry.

Because thinking about myself was too much.

I pictured him paying for his day with spoons — tiny invisible tokens he handed over for every task.

A spoon for therapy. A spoon for communicating what he wanted for lunch. Two spoons for transitions. Three spoons for anything unexpected.

And the only way he got spoons back was sleep... or the banana show.

By bedtime, he had nothing left. So, he either borrowed from tomorrow or fell apart.

I didn't realise I'd said it out loud until Tom blinked at me.

"That's... actually a really good way to put it," he said with surprise.

Angela overheard and stepped closer. "Jace, that's a brilliant analogy. You should share that with the group."

My stomach dropped.

I didn't want to share. I didn't want attention. I didn't want praise.

I felt like I was on an operating table and someone had cracked my chest open — my heart exposed, failing, blood pooling everywhere — and everyone was politely waiting for me to explain the carnage.

I wanted to deflect, but everyone was looking at me, and my usual charm seemed to be failing.

So, I repeated it — the spoons, the paying, the borrowing from tomorrow — and the room nodded like I'd said something wise.

Angela smiled warmly. "That's exactly it. Beautifully put."

Beautifully put.

If only she knew I wasn't talking about Harry.

I was talking about myself.

But I couldn't say that. Couldn't even think it without something inside me tightening like a fist.

Because if I admitted it — even silently — then I'd have to face the truth:

I was out of spoons. Had been for months. And I'd been borrowing from tomorrow so long I wasn't sure I had any of tomorrow's spoons left to borrow.

The group kept talking — spoons, buckets, burnout, Mickey's posts — but it all blurred.

Their voices felt far away.

All I could hear was my own heartbeat, loud and uneven, like it was trying to warn me of something I didn't want to name.

Angela passed around worksheets. "Write down one thing you do for yourself each week."

The room went quiet.

Tom stared at his blank page. Priya chewed her pen. Martha didn't even pick hers up.

Sarah wrote something, crossed it out, wrote something else, crossed that out too.

And I realised something.

These people — these parents — were drowning. Quietly. Constantly. And they didn't know how to come up for air.

I didn't either.

Angela sighed. "Self-care isn't selfish. It's survival. And if you don't do it, burnout will do it for you."

The group nodded, but no one looked convinced.

As the session wrapped up, I collected Harry because Liam and Anna were deep in conversation — in a good way, by the looks of it. I did my best to be the uncle he needed as I took him back to his parents. I needed to talk to someone, but Liam needed to focus on Anna right now. Then I overheard Sarah.

"I emailed Mickey from the link on her website yesterday and she sent me some information and references to other blogs who talk about it," Sarah chirped to Priya as she walked past.

For the briefest second, I thought, *I could talk to her. She wouldn't know who I was. I'd never have to see her again.*

But the thought evaporated as quickly as it came.

Harry tugged me toward the slide, and I let him pull me away — grateful for the distraction, terrified of the silence that would come without it.

Chapter Fourteen

The Morning That Went Sideways

Not every moment has to make sense. Sometimes surviving the chaos is the victory.

Mickey's Blog Bits

Jace

Anna had barely finished saying, “If you could just get Harry started while I shower—” before she disappeared down the hallway like someone fleeing a crime scene.

I stood in the kitchen, hands on hips, staring at Harry.

He stared back.

We were two cowboys in a standoff, except one of us was five and wearing dinosaur pyjamas.

“Alright, buddy,” I said in a Texan drawl. “Let’s get dressed.” I hold out my hand, he holds it tentatively, looking up at me as if I'm going to lasso him at any moment. I wink at him and start herding him towards his bedroom.

He got undressed easily and put on his underwear, giving me a false sense of success.

Then Harry stared up at me, “Dye-Dye.”

“Dinosaur?” I repeated, grabbing the dinosaur socks. “Got it.”

I knelt down and started putting them on.

Harry's whole body went rigid.

"Noh," he whispered.

I froze. "What do you mean, no? You said dinosaur."

He shook his head violently. "Pan."

"Okay," I said, trying to stay calm. "I'll put your pants on in a minute."

Harry kicked. Hard.

"NOH PAN!"

I blinked. "I know you said pants!"

He kicked again, louder this time. "No-no PAN. PAN!"

I stared at him, confused. "I'll just get this sock on and then we'll do pants."

He stomped his foot. "No-no. 'GAIN."

"What again?"

"'Gain!" he cried, pointing at the door.

His body tightened. His skin flushed red. His breathing quickened — fast, shallow, panicked.

I reached out to calm him, but he dropped to the floor and scrambled under the bed.

"'GAIN!" he yelled, voice cracking.

I stood there, useless, watching his little feet kick the underside of the mattress. I wanted to help. I just didn't know how. It felt like everyone else knew the rules of this world except me.

Anna came running down the hall. "What happened?"

"I don't know — he said pants, then I said I'd do it soon, then he said again and pointed at the door and now he's under the bed."

Anna's voice softened in a way I hadn't mastered yet — steady, warm, certain. "Harry, sweetheart, come out please. We'll put your pants on first."

"'GAIN!" Harry screamed, kicking harder.

Anna closed her eyes for a moment — gathering strength from somewhere deep — then pulled out her phone.

I watched her thumb scroll through her contacts until she tapped Kayla and hit call.

Of course. When things went sideways, you called someone who understood sideways.

I leaned back against the wall, rubbing my face. B*et her morning's running like clockwork,* I thought.

Kayla

I was already up and heading toward the kitchen when the music went off — "Thunder, ah-ah, ah-ah-ah."

I turned the corner and froze.

"Breathe. Just breathe," I told myself.

The floor was covered in hundreds and thousands. A rainbow crime scene.

And then I smelled it — the unmistakable smell of poo drifting down the hallway.

Violet entered from the other side and took one look at my face.

"Do you want me to sweep it up?"

It wasn't fair to her. She was still a kid. I'd always tried to protect her from taking on too much responsibility too early.

But God, I was blessed to have her.

"Thanks, sweetheart. I better go check on your brother."

I headed down the hallway to Archie's room. My heart lifted the moment I saw him. He stared up at me, soiled cloths in his hand. Yes, there was a mess — but he had tried so hard to clean up his own accident. He looked so disappointed in himself.

I knelt down and smiled. "You're such a good boy. You tried to clean it up. Thank you. Let's get you showered and then Mummy will finish cleaning."

As I washed him, I thought about how people would judge me for not disciplining him for the sprinkles. It's easy to judge from the outside. But I've learned to focus on the triumphs, not kill myself over every battle.

Had there not been a mess in his bedroom, it would've been different. But right now, all I could see was a little boy trying his best.

Suddenly Archie grabbed the shower head and sprayed me.

"Oh, two can play at this game," I laughed, turning it back on him.

Five minutes later we emerged still giggling. I gathered up the soiled bedding, helped him with his shirt and left him to put on the rest of his school clothes.

I'd barely reached the kitchen to make lunch when my phone rang.

"Hi Anna, everything okay?"

She filled me in on the morning's events.

I smiled to myself.

Mornings!

Jace

Anna hung up the phone. Harry had calmed down, but he still wouldn't come out.

"Harry," she said gently, "if you come out from under the bed, you can show me where you want to start your day again. Okay?"

Harry slowly poked his head out. He seemed to trust what she was saying. He crawled out, pulled off the sock, climbed back into bed, and closed his eyes.

I looked at Anna. I had never gotten him out of bed before.

"Do you want Mum to say it or Uncle Jace?"

After a beat, he cracked one eye open.

"On kuh Jay."

"Say what?" I asked.

"The wake-up," Harry demanded.

Anna whispered, "Say 'Good morning.'"

I cleared my throat. "Good morning, Harry."

He sat up instantly, cheerful as sunshine. "GOOD MORNING ON KUH JAY!"

We started again.

This time, Anna showed me the correct order, and I put the pants on first. Then the socks. Then the shirt. Then the jumper.

Perfect.

I exhaled in triumph.

"Dih?" Harry asked.

"Sure, what drink do you want?"

"Boo Kuh."

Easy. I walked to the kitchen, with Harry one step behind me.

I opened the cupboard.

No blue cup.

I checked the sink.

No blue cup.

I checked the dishwasher.

No blue cup.

I checked the fridge for reasons I cannot explain.

Still no blue cup. I turned towards him.

"Harry," I said carefully, "where did you last see your blue cup?"

He shrugged. "Boo kuh."

Right. Yes. That's... helpful.

I opened every cupboard like I was searching for hidden treasure.

I found:

- a green cup
- a cup that was kind of blue but apparently "NOH BOO!"
- a green cup with dinosaurs
- a cup with glitter
- a cup that looked like it had been through a war

But no blue cup.

Harry followed me around chanting, "Boo kuh. Boo kuh. BOO KUH," like a tiny cult leader.

I tried offering the green cup.

He recoiled like I'd handed him a live snake.

"NOH GEEN. BOO CUP."

"Okay, okay," I muttered, checking behind the toaster, under the couch cushions, inside a shoe (don't ask).

Nothing.

Then I opened the freezer.

And there it was.

The blue cup. Sitting proudly between the frozen peas and a packet of chips.

I held it up like a trophy. "FOUND IT!"

Harry beamed. "BOO KUH!"

I filled it with water and handed it to him.

He took a sip, nodded once, and said, "Bef iss." I sighed with relief.

"Okay, let's wait for Mum. Wanna watch the banana show?"

He nodded excitedly. I put it on and collapsed into a chair.

Anna walked out of the hallway, hair wet, looking refreshed and peaceful.

"How'd it go?" she asked.

I stared at her.

She stared back.

Then she laughed. "Oh no. What happened now?"

I pointed at Harry. "The blue cup was in the freezer."

"Yeah — oops, I forgot to mention," she said casually. "He likes it cold."

I put my head in my hands. "I'm not built for this."

Anna patted my shoulder. "You're learning."

Harry climbed into my lap, blue cup in hand, and leaned against me like it was the most natural thing in the world.

And just like that, with Harry warm against me and his cold blue cup pressed to his chest, the chaos didn't feel like failure anymore.

It felt like something I would treasure forever.

The feeling twisted inside me — warm and sharp at the same time.

Because moments like this... they healed something in me. Made me feel useful. Needed. Like I still had a place in this world, even if it wasn't the one I'd imagined for myself.

But they also reminded me of everything I'd lost. Everything I might never have. Everything I'd quietly accepted I didn't get to want anymore.

Holding Harry felt like breathing again. But it also felt like standing outside a window, watching a life I wasn't sure I was allowed to step into.

And I didn't know what to do with that. Not yet.

Chapter Fifteen

Binding Rules

Some rules protect us. Some rules trap us. The hardest part is realising which ones we wrote ourselves.

Mickey's Blog Bits

Jace

I should've been asleep.

The Predators had shut out the Wolves, Liam was snoring on the other end of the couch, and the house was finally quiet.

But my mind wasn't. I couldn't bring myself to go to bed.

I kept replaying the morning — Harry melting down, the blue cup in the freezer, Anna knowing exactly what to do while I stood there like an idiot. And then the parent group. The spoons. The rules. The feeling I'd been trying not to name.

So instead of sleeping, I pulled out my phone and opened *Our Autistic Journey*.

I could see why the parents connected to it. They weren't just reading a blog — they were reading about themselves. Post after post. Story after story. Honest. Raw. Funny in places. Painful in others.

When I finally glanced at my watch, it was 1:30 a.m.

Two hours. I'd been reading for two hours.

But one thing stuck with me more than anything else — the rules.

The way Mickey described them. The way they shaped her life. The way they sounded nothing like Harry's rigidity... and yet somehow exactly like it.

Was that what the blue cup was? A rule?

Were restrictive behaviours just... rules?

I scrolled to the bottom of the page and saw the contact email Sarah had mentioned.

My thumb hovered over it.

I could ask the group next week. I could leave it alone. I could pretend I wasn't thinking about this at all.

But the truth was, I *was* thinking about it. Too much.

A tiny, stupid part of me whispered: *She doesn't know you. You don't know her. Why would she care?*

Another part — the part that had been rattled all day — whispered back: *Because you need to understand this.*

I exhaled, thumb still frozen above the screen.

What the hell.

Couldn't hurt to ask.

I typed a message and hit send.

To my surprise, a reply came back in less than a minute.

Jace & Mickey (online messaging)

J: So… I was thinkin' about your blog. And about my nephew. He's really rigid about stuff — routines, rules, has to have his blue cup for a drink or it's the end of the world. Were your rules kinda the same thing?

M: Partly, yes. But not entirely.

J: What d'you mean?

M: I'm not an expert but I guess, his rigidity is likely neurological. Mine was…More of a trauma response dressed up as a personality.

J: Dressed up how?

M: I created a character. An identity I thought everyone wanted.

Every day I was acting out this version of myself, and the world was my stage.

J: I heard you'd taught English …but Shakespeare, really.

M: L.O.L. I never even realised.

J: Alright. So… were you ever yourself, Mickey?

M: I don't know. Honestly, I don't think I knew who "myself" was. I just knew who I *shouldn't* be. Too loud. Too emotional. Too noticeable. Too… me.

J: Damn. It sounds like you were tryin' to hide.

M: I did in order to survive. And I dulled myself in the process. My creativity. My instincts. My voice. All the parts of me that didn't fit the character I'd built.

Jace: And now?

Mickey: Now I can look back at ten-year-old me and laugh a little. Not at her pain — never that. But at the rules themselves.

They were so dramatic. So absolute. So… biblical.

Jace: Biblical?

Mickey: Oh yes. I basically wrote my own commandments.

Jace: Alright, now I gotta hear this.

Mickey: Fine. But you asked to see this side of me. Where is it, I wrote it down earlier — imagine a dramatic voice.

Thou shalt not wear bright colours. For they draw the eye, and the eye bringeth judgement.

Thou shalt remain in the shadows. Corners, edges, behind taller people — blessed be the blind spots.

Thou shalt speak only when thou hast rehearsed. Improvisation is the devil's playground.

Thou shalt flee when the conversation strays from the sacred script. Yea, even unto the bathroom if necessary.

Thou shalt not engage with boys in the presence of girls. For jealousy is swift and terrifying.

Thou shalt not be loud, bold, noticeable, or memorable. Blend, child. Blend like the wind.

Above all, thou shalt not give anyone a reason to leave. For rejection is death to the nervous system.

L.O.L Needs some work still.

Jace: ...Mickey.

Reading her rules did something to me — something I wasn't ready for.

Because they weren't my rules, not really. But the feeling behind them... the way she shaped herself to survive... the way she shrank to fit the world... I knew that feeling.

Not in the same way, or anywhere near the same level and certainly not for the same reasons. But I'd built my own commandments too.

Don't complain. Don't show weakness. Don't talk about the injury. Don't talk about the coaching accident. Don't talk about the future you lost. Don't want things you can't have. Don't let anyone see you fall apart.

Rules I never wrote down. Rules I never questioned. Rules that kept me moving... and kept me stuck.

And suddenly it wasn't just Harry's rigidity I was thinking about. It was how deeply that rigidity runs, how it protects him, how it serves a purpose even when the rest of us don't understand it.

I'd been fortunate. I could see why I became rigid, and I could change it if I wanted to. Harry can't. Archie can't. Their brains don't function the same way mine does — and that's not wrong. It's just different.

I thought about what Kayla said — how one of Archie's schools tried to stop his hand-flapping. It was the first time I'd ever seen her angry. Really angry. She said it didn't matter if anyone understood it; the flapping helped him. It wasn't hurting him or anyone else, so they could shove their opinions where the sun doesn't shine.

Her exact words. I swear.

J: Mickey what about a boy who wants nothing but a blue cup.

M: Well you have two choices, buy a lot of the exact same blue cup and make sure you take it with you everywhere; not exactly practical. Or on the days when the child is regulated and happy, that's the day you stretch.

J: Stretch?

M: Yes stretch. You give them a blue cup that is different. A different colour or shape. Then along the way you change it to a green cup or purple cup. But you do it in their time when they are able. Just a little bit of stretch in another direction not a forced change.

J: What about hand flapping?

M: Hand flapping is not rigidity – it is a repetitive movement that provides an outlet for the nervous system. In my opinion it would be like telling you that you are not allowed to blink if a ball is thrown at your face.

J: Yeah you got me there. Did you get rid of your rules by stretching?

M: Yes and No. My rules began in childhood from people who made me feel worthless. Truth be told I still catch myself following the rules even now.

J: Mickey …

M: Yes?

J: You didn't deserve to feel like that. And you sure as hell didn't deserve to feel like you had to disappear.

I stared at the screen for a long moment. She didn't need to answer. She'd already said more than most people ever do.

I set my phone down and let my head fall back against the couch. The room felt too quiet — the kind of quiet that makes you hear your own thoughts whether you want to or not.

I wasn't falling apart. Not yet. But I wasn't fine either.

And for the first time, it hit me that maybe it was time to confront what I'd been avoiding.

She'd survived things I didn't have names for. She'd lived inside rules that made mine look simple. She noticed parts of the world I was only just beginning to notice.

Maybe it wasn't about finding someone to talk to at all. Maybe it was about finally being ready to face what was going on. Mickey hadn't asked anything of me, and I hadn't told her a damn thing about myself — but something in the way she saw the world made me look at my own differently.

I exhaled slowly.

Yeah. Maybe that was enough for tonight. Time to sleep.

Chapter Sixteen

It's Lonely on the Edge

Carrying a burden isn't the heavy part. Carrying it alone is.
Mickey's Blog Bits

Jace

Angela starts the session with a check-in. Priya goes first.

"I spoke to a lawyer yesterday," she says, blunt as ever. "I'm done. I'm doing everything alone. I'm exhausted. He thinks I should work, take care of the kids, and do all the house chores by myself. He makes no effort to understand the boys. If I wasn't already doing it alone, I might be scared of going alone, but..."

A few people nod. A few murmur sympathy. The room settles into that familiar heaviness — the kind that comes from people who are tired to the bone.

There was a moment of silence before she finished in a defeated tone, "I just feel so overwhelmed and alone."

Then Kayla speaks.

Her voice is soft at first, then steadier.

"I get it," she says. "Raising kids with disabilities is hard. Not because they're a burden — they're not! ... But living with a disability *is* hard. It affects every part of daily life. And pretending it doesn't only makes parents feel more alone."

The room goes still.

She takes a breath.

"But what makes it even harder is everything around the disability. The systems. The judgement. The lack of understanding. The way you have to fight for every tiny piece of support. The way even the kindest of people say, 'Let me know if you need anything,' but don't actually know how to help and you're too burnt out to tell them how."

A few parents nod. A few look like they might cry.

Kayla continues, almost shyly.

"Some days I feel like I'm doing everything wrong. Some days I feel like I'm doing everything alone. But then I come here, and I remember I'm not the only one trying to hold it together. I'm not the only one exhausted from advocating, or explaining, or being misunderstood."

She looks down at her hands, cheeks pink, like she regrets saying anything.

I can't look away.

Not because I'm drawn to her — though I am — but because she's saying the thing I've been circling for weeks:

It's lonely when you don't know how to help. It's lonelier when you're the one who needs help and don't know how to ask.

Kayla reaches across to Priya and squeezes her hand.

"We're here for you," she says. "All of us. And if you feel like you're doing it alone... you don't have to."

Tom echoes her words and shares how he's been struggling raising his grandson alone. The group softens, bonds over shared vulnerability.

And yeah, it's not the same, but I get the feeling of being alone when life doesn't go the way you planned. I don't have someone relying on me, but I know what it's like to feel like a spectator watching your life veer off course. To feel like you're the only one who doesn't know the rules.

I feel like these people get that. And I want to be part of it.

My eyes drift back to Kayla, even though she's not talking anymore.

But she still won't look at me.

When the session ends, people start packing up. Anna leans toward me.

“She's shy,” she whispers. “Don't take it personally.”

I shrug like I don't know who she means.

Shy is one thing. Avoiding me like I'm radioactive is another.

Kayla and Priya leave together, and I try to focus on asking Liam and Anna what they're doing next.

But as I walked toward them, I found myself watching Kayla go — drawn in by something I couldn't quite name, something heavier than simple curiosity.

A tightness pulled through my chest. Recognition. She carried more than she ever let show. And for the first time, I saw it — the weight she held, the way she kept moving anyway.

Maybe that was why I kept looking. Sure, there was an attraction there — I wasn't blind — but that wasn't what pulled at me. It was the instinct to stand beside her, to shield her from whatever had made her so damn strong.

I couldn't go there. I knew that. I had enough of my own mess to sort out.

But wanting to protect her? Wanting to make things a little easier for her, even if she never knew? Yeah. That felt right. That felt like something I should do.

Just like helping with Harry felt right. It made me feel useful again, like I still had something to offer. But Harry also reminded me of everything I'd lost — everything I'd quietly decided I didn't get to want anymore.

Maybe that was why watching her walk away hit harder than it should. Not because I wanted anything from her, but because I understood her now in a way I hadn't before. And I wasn't sure I had the strength to let anyone understand me back.

Everyone here is fighting something. She's no exception. And the last thing she needs is someone dragging her down.

If this was ever meant to be more… I'd need more support than I've been willing to admit.

Chapter Seventeen

Two Kids, One Heart, Nothing Left to Give

Autistic people don't lack empathy or love. If anything, they feel both too deeply, just not always in ways the world recognises.
Mickey's Blog Bits

Kayla

It's a typical Saturday morning.

Archie is in the living room watching his shows. Well—watching, pacing, sitting, standing, pacing again. His usual rhythm.

Violet is in her room playing computer games. Today she has a friend over — Aleia. Sweet kid. Cheeky, extroverted, a ball of sunshine. The kind of child who pulls Violet out of her shell without even trying.

I'm chugging coffee like it's the magical elixir of life.

Yesterday I was a little too honest in the parent group, mentioning my IVF sperm-donor journey and how there was a time I wondered if I would have made the same decisions about having the kids if I knew what I know now. I always felt guilty that those thoughts had even crossed my mind, even for a second. The conversations have been looping in my head ever since. I hope people understood they were fleeting. I love my kids. I don't regret a thing.

I think intrusive Trudy snuck in the back door. I didn't mention her in the parent group when I explained how my brain works, but she's been around for years — a frenemy of the triplets and best mates with overthinking Owen. I spent five years learning to catch her in the act and shut her down. Every time she started whispering the same toxic rubbish, I'd drown her out with opposing songs or scripture until my brain finally built its own alarm system. Most days it works. Today... she slipped through. But I'm not letting her stay.

So what if some mornings I wake up and wonder what my life would've looked like if I'd waited. If I'd ignored the doctors. Ignored the timelines. Ignored the fear of losing the chance to be a mum.

It never lasts long, because Archie will give me that cheeky smile, or Violet will share her passions and dreams, and the thought dissolves. And it's never about them, it's about my insecurities and feelings of inadequacy.

I made my choice. I'd make it again.

The girls have moved into the living room. They're giggling over something on Violet's iPad when Aleia pauses.

"Who's that guy?" she asks, pointing at a photo on the table.

I poke my head around the corner—and my stomach drops.

It's a photo from the day Harry and Jace came over to bake. A record of the chaos and flour and laughter.

And there he is. Jace. Smiling. Warm. Effortlessly handsome in a way that annoys me more than it should. This is the one area I can control.

Violet answers before I can move.

"That's Harry's uncle."

Aleia grins. "He's cute. Is he your mum's boyfriend?"

I almost drop my cup.

"Mum's friend Anna was trying to set them up, I think," Violet says, matter-of-fact.

Violet glances at me — quick, sharp, too knowing for her age. She knows I never date. Never talk about men. Never even look.

I hope I haven't screwed up her future relationships.

I keep pretending I'm fine. Unaffected. Neutral.

But my brain is already spiralling.

I have always loved too hard and too fast. In friendships. In dating. In everything.

It doesn't matter how much therapy I've had. It doesn't matter how many rules I've built. It doesn't matter how much I try to stay steady.

It grows anyway.

It's the reason I avoid relationships. The reason I keep my distance. The reason I don't look Jace in the eye for more than a second.

I don't fall in love. I fall into obsession. Into fantasy. Into a version of someone that isn't real.

And when reality hits, it destroys me.

I can't do that again. Not with two kids depending on me. Not with a life built out of routines and safety and predictability.

But God, I wish I wasn't so bad at relationships. I wish I knew how to let people in without tearing myself apart.

I grip the bench so hard my knuckles ache.

A sudden cry — sharp, panicked — followed by the sound of a head hitting something hard comes from the lounge, yanking me from my spiralling thoughts.

I rush back in and find Archie on the floor, screaming — the high-pitched, panicked kind that means something tipped him over the edge. Violet freezes, and Aleia is trying to calm him, but he flails and hits her arm. She pulls back, overwhelmed.

I'm already moving — and apologising.

"Sorry — he needs space when he's upset like this. Can you pass me his blanket? Did you see what happened?"

Aleia shakes her head, wide-eyed. But when I look toward the TV, I see it.

A character he loves is in trouble on the screen.

Of course.

He is full of empathy. It doesn't matter how many times he's seen these cartoons — he still cries when he thinks someone else is scared or hurt.

I sit beside him, draping the blanket over his shoulders, stroking his back through the fabric.

“Violet,” I say gently.

She snaps into focus, stepping closer.

“It’s okay, sweetheart,” I tell her. She loves him, but she doesn’t know how to handle him. Sometimes it frustrates her. Sometimes it angers her. Sometimes it overwhelms her.

She kneels beside us, voice soft. “It’s okay, Archie.”

Eventually Archie’s breathing slows. Violet strokes his hair — hesitant at first, then gentle.

He lets her.

A tiny miracle.

He leans into her touch. She smiles, soft and proud.

For a moment, they’re just siblings. Not diagnoses. Not challenges. Just two kids who love each other in the only ways they know how.

My heart aches with it.

I squeeze Violet’s hand. Then Archie’s.

Two kids. One heart. Mine.

And there’s no room left for anything else. Not for longing. Not for wanting. Not for a man with kind eyes and a wickedly charming smile.

I can’t afford feelings. My kids need all of me.

Even the broken parts.

Chapter Eighteen

Different Operating Systems, Same Playground

Autistic brains aren't broken versions of neurotypical ones — they're different operating systems entirely. Connection happens when someone learns your interface instead of insisting you run their software.

Mickey's Blog Bits

Kayla

We arrive early to the parent-group park meet-up. Archie is already on the swing, soaring back and forward in rhythmic bliss. Violet is climbing to the top of the fort, staking her claim as queen of the kingdom below.

I sit on the bench watching a Fern Brady clip on my phone. For the fifteenth time.

I haven't followed Fern Brady much, but two things she's said have stuck with me. First, no one talks about how weird neurotypical people are. Second more neutrality is needed when describing autism, not as a superpower and not as a tragedy> But as a different operating system like iOS and android.

I still find her delivery funny. Still painfully accurate.

I ponder ...

If neurotypical and autistic minds are different operating systems, then autistic minds aren't one OS — they're a whole collection of niche systems, custom-built, patched, jailbroken, and occasionally held together with sensory tape.

And this park meet-up? It's a tech convention where nothing syncs and everyone's Bluetooth is on.

Archie is running experimental firmware powered by swings, puddles, and white foods. Violet is a privacy-focused minimalist OS that crashes if you open too many tabs at once. And I'm the Windows PC with seventeen tabs open, six incomplete Word documents, three Excel sheets, and twenty unread emails and yet somehow I'm still functioning.

And every other person who will be here today — autistic, ADHD, AuDHD, or other forms of neurodivergence — are running something entirely different. It makes sense really. I mean we are different neurologically. Neurotypical people just happen to fit the mould.

My thoughts are interrupted when Harry comes sprinting across the park, banana toy held high like a warrior wielding a sword as they charge into battle. Anna and Jace trail behind him, already apologising for nothing in particular.

Two of Priya's kids — Joshua and Thinley — zoom past like twin comets. Noah and Dale wander over more slowly with their mothers.

In the distance, I hear Tom talking to Martha and Janette, who have just arrived.

Within minutes, the parents have set up picnic blankets and camping chairs. Shoes come off. Sunscreen is slathered on children who behave like greased eels.

Then the kids scatter.

Instant mayhem.

Joshua is halfway up a tree. Dale is standing on the picnic blanket like it's a lifeboat and the grass is lava. Archie is watching everything from the swing like a sitting judge. Violet is observing from the fort, silently avoiding the chaos. Noah has wandered beyond the playground boundaries, staring at clouds. Allira sits just beyond the adults with her headphones on, radiating teenage goth energy.

Harry, Thinley, Louise, and Arden gather at the slide. The parents have settled into their seats, after all this is nothing new. But Jace looks overwhelmed till he realises no one else is concerned. He looks over to the slide, shrugs and sits down.

Harry slides down first. Then immediately becomes the Slide Police.
"WAY. WAY. NOH GOH. NA-NA TUH."
He holds up the banana toy like a traffic baton.

Thinley tries to push past him.

Harry screams. Arden, sweet gentle Arden, steps in front of her — raptor toy clutched in his fist.

"Thinley, you have to wait," he says earnestly. "Banana hasn't had a turn."

Thinley glares at him.

Arden straightens, takes a breath, and lets out a determined little dinosaur roar — more turkey-raptor than terrifying, but full of conviction.

Then, with absolute seriousness:

"I'm the Giganotosaurus. Apex dinosaur. You have to listen."

Thinley freezes, startled.

Arden nods once, satisfied.
Head dinosaur status: established.

Harry climbs back up the ladder, panting dramatically.

"AH-ee dow," he instructs Arden, "Na-na GOH!"

Arden nods solemnly. He is a child who takes rules seriously. Even banana-related ones.

Harry reaches the bottom and shouts, "GOH!"

Arden releases the banana. It shoots down the slide like a tiny yellow missile and lands in Harry's arms.

Louise narrates loudly, "AND BANANA SCORES A PERFECT LANDING!"

This continues for several rounds until Thinley snaps.

She shoves her way up the fort stairs and over the platform to the top of the slide, pushes Arden aside, and takes a turn that is absolutely not hers.

Harry screams. Arden clutches his side where she pushed him, whispering, "That was a carnivore move." Louise bursts into tears.

The crying sets off Archie on the swing. Then Harry again. Then Thinley, because everyone else is crying.

The parents move like a well-trained emergency response team.

Priya abandons her battle with Dale's shoes and runs toward Thinley. Anna is already with Harry. Tom checks on Arden. Janette scoops up Louise. I'm at the swing trying to calm Archie, knowing nothing will settle him until the crying stops.

Eventually, the chaos settles.

We gather the kids on the rug for snacks.

Violet, Noah, and Alex drift over slowly, drawn by the gravitational pull of food.

Priya looks around and realises Joshua is still in the tree.

"Joshua! Come get snacks!"

"No."

"Joshua, come down."

"No. I live here now."

"Joshua—"

"I AM ONE WITH THE TREE."

Meanwhile, Thinley is quietly stealing snacks from her brothers. Arden notices.

His sense of justice ignites.

"Thinley, you OVIRAPTOR, STOP STEALING! THAT IS NOT FAIR!"

He stands, pointing dramatically like a tiny lawyer.

Tom tries to settle him. Sarah tries to settle Thinley. Priya is still negotiating with the tree-dweller.

Archie starts typing on his communication device:

TOO LOUD. TOO LOUD. TOO LOUD.

Allira pulls her hoodie over her head and retreats further away.

Violet, Alex, and Noah take their snacks to a table across the way. They sit together but do not speak. Just three quiet kids eating in parallel like a peaceful little neurodivergent council. Once Thinley has all her extra snacks removed Arden joins them,

Once everyone is fed, I walk over to Violet, Alex and Arden. People often underestimate them, but they're fantastic leaders, I have seen each of them organise and guide the younger kids before.

“Would you two be able to run some games for the younger kids? Duck Duck Goose? What’s the Time Mr Wolf?”

Violet nods with the seriousness of someone accepting a military assignment. Alex salutes. Arden declares he will be a Utahraptor to Violet's T-Rex, which I think translates to he will be her right hand.

They gather the younger kids on the grass — even Dale, who has put his shoes on and brought his personal towel to sit on.

The games begin.

The rules... do not survive.

“Duck Duck Goose” becomes “Duck Duck Dinosaur.” “What’s the Time Mr Wolf?” becomes “What’s the Time Mr Banana?” Thinley keeps changing the rules mid-game. Harry keeps enforcing rules no one agreed to. Joshua keeps running off. Arden keeps correcting everyone’s dinosaur facts. Louise narrates every moment like a live broadcast.

And somehow — somehow — it works.

Even Allira eventually wanders over to help.

The parents finally get to sit, breathe, and talk.

We watch the chaos with the kind of fond amusement that only comes from surviving it daily.

This is our life.

Messy.

Loud.

Chaotic.

Funny.

Different.

Beautiful.

Not a tragedy. Not a superpower.

Just different people with different operating systems— all trying their best— all learning each other's languages and all finding their place in the world.

And honestly?

I wouldn't trade it for anything.

Chapter Nineteen

Trying Too Hard

You don't have to be the hero every day. Sometimes the bravest thing you can do is admit you're drowning and let someone throw you a rope.

Mickey's Blog Bits

Jace

I'm trying. God, I'm trying so hard.

The parent group had been on break for the holidays, but at the park meet-up I basically cornered everyone. I asked a hundred questions. They gave me a few things to try — keep my voice steady, don't rise to the yelling, say things the same way each time, breathe, redirect. I don't know. I'm trying. That's all I've got.

I wrote them down. I practised them. I rehearsed them in the mirror like an idiot.

And today I tried one.

It went badly.

Harry wanted the blue cup. The blue cup was in the dishwasher.

Last time, I'd said, "Start again?" and he'd reset like a little robot rebooting.

So I tried it again.

"Start again, buddy?"

He screamed like I'd stabbed him.

Then he threw the red cup at my shin. Then he cried because he threw the cup. Then he cried because he was crying. Then he cried because I existed.

And I stood there thinking, I'm the adult. I should know how to do this. Why don't I know how to do this?

I tried the script.

"I hear you. You want the blue cup. The blue cup is dirty. You can choose the red cup or the green cup."

He screamed louder.

Then I remember the conversation with Mickey – stretch him when he's regulated. Guess I need to find a few more identical blue cups until that time comes.

By the time he finally calmed down, I felt like I'd run a marathon in a strait-jacket.

I stepped into the laundry, shut the door, and leaned my forehead against the wall.

Just for a minute. Just to breathe. Just to not fall apart in front of my nephew.

And then the thought hit me — sharp, ugly, honest:

Maybe it's a blessing I can't have kids. Because clearly I'd be terrible at it.

It punched the air out of my lungs.

Kayla does this every day. Anna does this every day. They stay calm. They stay steady. Meanwhile I'm falling apart over a cup.

How do they do it? How do they keep going? Because right now I feel like I could sleep for a week.

I didn't want to ask Liam for help. He's finally doing better. Anna's back. He's lighter. Happier. He doesn't need my crap dragging him down.

But I needed something. Anything. So I pulled out my phone.

I'd read so many of her blogs. I'd thought about messaging her more times than I'd admit. The anonymous blogger who writes about anxiety and masking and therapy and all the things I don't know how to say out loud.

She doesn't know me. She'll never meet me. It felt... safe.

So I messaged Mickey.

> **J:** I have been reading your blog. I am helping my brother with my nephew. They suspect Autism. You wrote about depression, anxiety. I need someone to talk to?

Send. Regret. Why did I mention depression? Fix it.

> **J:** I'm trying so hard but I feel like I'm making everything worse. I came here 'cause my life was in limbo and now I think I'm no help here either.

Send. More regret. That was worse. So much worse.

> **J:** You don't have to reply but I hope to hear from you.

Send. Better. Maybe.

What was I doing? Why was I dumping my feelings on a stranger? Why was I acting like some lost kid?

No reply came.

Of course it didn't. Why would she reply? She probably gets messages like that all the time. Or maybe she read it and thought I was pathetic.

Five years ago I wasn't like this. Back then I was twenty-eight, captain of my team, playing the best hockey of my life, on the verge of winning a major trophy. I'd been in the NHL since I was twenty-one. Seven seasons. Seven years of pressure and glory and noise and purpose.

Then the injury hit — fast, brutal, final. My career ended overnight. Everything I'd built my life around disappeared.

I clawed my way back as a skills development coach. Five years of rebuilding. Five years of being good at something again. Five years of feeling like I had a place in the world. I met Mel. Life steadied.

And then came the second setback — the accident on the ice. I told management he wasn't ready for certain modes of play. He could read the puck better than anyone, but he couldn't read the other players, and that's dangerous when the game tips from rough to reckless.

Now he's lucky to be alive, even if he'll spend the rest of his life in a wheelchair., and I can't block out that accident or the flashbacks of my own.

The ice used to be my refuge — my stillness in a world full of pressure — and now I avoid it.

I shoved my phone in my pocket and walked back into the lounge.

Liam was on the couch, scrolling his phone. He looked up instantly.

"What's wrong?"

"Nothing," I said. "Just tired."

He didn't buy it. He never buys it.

His eyes flicked toward the kitchen. "Harry had a rough one?"

"Yeah."

"You okay?"

"Yeah," I lied.

He studied me for a second, then sighed — not annoyed, not judging, just... seeing me.

"You're carrying something heavy," he said quietly. "You don't have to pretend you're fine."

I didn't deny it. I didn't know how.

I just sat there, feeling like a man who keeps trying to climb out of a hole only to slide back down again.

And I kept feeling stupid for wanting things I have no business wanting.

Chapter Twenty

Two Offers

Sometimes life hands you two choices at once — the one you wanted and the one you needed. And the hardest part isn't choosing between them. It's admitting you're scared of both.

Mickey's Blog Bits

Jace

I wake up feeling like I didn't sleep at all. Head thick. Chest tight. Thoughts slow and sharp at the same time — terrible mix.

I check my phone. Still nothing from Mickey.

Writing to her was supposed to be easier than talking to my family. Safer. Less... exposing.

I drag myself into the kitchen. Liam and Anna are laughing about something. Harry's lining up his toast crusts by size.

I feel like a moocher taking up space.

My phone buzzes. Probably spam.

No. It's her.

Mickey.

My stomach drops.

I open the message.

Hi Jace, Thank you for trusting me with this. I'm honoured you felt safe enough to reach out. If you want to talk about strategies for supporting your nephew like we have before, I'm happy to share what I've learned .... But because you mentioned depression and feeling stuck, I really want to encourage you to speak with a counsellor or therapist if you can... *Therapy made a huge difference for me — not every therapist was the right fit, but the right ones helped me rebuild myself when I didn't know how. I can't really write about it now but I've written about accessing therapy and my own experiences in these posts: "Not Everyone Will Listen," "Attacking Anxiety Back," and "Schemes, Sacrifice and Self-Identity".* ...Take care. —M

I stare at the screen. My chest loosens — just a little — like someone cracked a window.

She didn't ignore me. Didn't brush me off.

But... therapist?

Do I need a therapist again?

I saw one for the PTSD, but...

I don't know. I don't know anything right now.

Relief mixes with embarrassment. I feel exposed but seen.

And that last one... yeah. That's the one that gets under my skin.

I read the message again. And again.

My email pings.

An assistant coaching offer. Seattle. Good job.

Great pay.

In something I used to be good at.

A position with decision making power. A real future.

I should feel excited. I should feel something.

Instead it feels like standing on a cliff with no idea which path is safest.

I close the email. Put my phone down. Try to breathe.

Later, I take Harry to the park.

He's on the swing, legs pumping, hair flying everywhere.

"On-kuh Jay, my uh?" he asks, frowning pointing at my mouth. I couldn't help smiling. We'd ended up at the same park where the parent group met last Saturday.

"Just thinking about the park visit with all your friends last weekend."

"Fuh!" he squeals. "Na-na go 'gain. 'Gain eh day."

"It was fun, Harry."

He bores of the swing and bolts toward the slide. I'm grateful when I see I'm not expected to help banana take his turns. The sky grows dark.

"Time to go Harry," I call out,

"Moh," he demands.

"Alright. One more minute or five more slides."

"Fy moh lies!" he yells, already climbing.

I'm getting better at this.

But the hollow feeling's still there, sitting heavy in my chest.

Chapter Twenty-One

The Mask Cracks

Masking doesn't crack because you're weak. It cracks because you've been holding the world together with your bare hands for too long.
Mickey's Blog Bits

Kayla

Violet walks into the kitchen and I know instantly she's unsettled. Not sick. Not grumpy. Just... a ball of anxiety waiting for the smallest tug.

Her shoulders are up around her ears. Her voice is flat. Her movements are stiff, careful — like she's trying not to touch the world too hard.

Masking fatigue.

I know the signs. The quiet ones. The ones no one else sees.

She sits at the table and stares at her cereal like it's a test she didn't study for.

"Sweetheart, you okay?"

She nods. Too fast. Too sharp.

Archie watches her from the couch, already picking up the shift in the air. He feels emotions like weather fronts.

I keep the morning routine exactly the same. Same breakfast. Same order. Same steps. More time.

But it only takes one tiny thing.

The blue water bottle isn't in the fridge. It's in the sink.

That's all it takes.

Violet freezes. Her breath stutters. Her eyes go glassy.

Then the meltdown hits — quiet, fast, devastating.

Crying. Shaking. Hiding behind her hands. Shutting down like a computer crash.

Archie panics instantly. He runs to her, then away, then back again, flapping his hands, making distressed little sounds. Her sadness hurts him like it's happening to him.

"I've got her, sweetheart," I tell him gently. "Go watch Sesame Street."

He hesitates, then obeys, still glancing back.

I'm pulled in two directions again. Violet curled in on herself. Archie overwhelmed by her overwhelm.

Two kids. Two different needs. Both urgent. Both mine.

I kneel beside Violet, rubbing her back in slow circles — the way she likes.

"It's okay. You're okay. I've got you."

The little empath doesn't stay away for long. Archie returns and presses his forehead against my arm, needing contact, needing reassurance, needing me.

I wish I could split myself in two. Instead, I feel like I'm failing both of them.

"Sweetheart," I say softly, "I'm just going to finish Archie's lunch and get him on the bus. You stay home for a while. If you feel up to school later, you can go. If not, you can stay home all day."

This isn't a sick day. It's a mental health day.

Sending her would only make everything worse.

She nods without lifting her head.

I cuddle Archie, finish his lunch, and lead him out when the bus arrives.

When I return, Violet hasn't moved much.

"Want to curl up on the lounge and watch a movie? I'll get the weighted blanket and make hot chocolate."

She nods again.

I don't push her to talk. She'll talk when she's ready.

We watch a movie. Slowly, her body unclenches.

"Do you want to go to school or stay home?" I ask quietly.

"Stay home," she whispers.

"Okay. Do you want me to organise a session with Jane? Or let her know you're having a rough day?"

I silently hope she says yes. Jane is the first counsellor Violet has ever really connected with, and the difference has been life-changing.

"I see her on the weekend, right?"

"Yes."

"I can wait till then."

Okay. Not Jane. Plan B, then.

Later, we walk to the park.

I'm still raw around the edges. I hate seeing my children upset. It's harder with Violet because she doesn't communicate with me the way she does with her counsellor or my sister.

At first that used to bother me — until I realised she's scared of disappointing me. Scared I'll see her differently.

It's ridiculous, but it's how she feels. And I have to let her work through that in her own time.

Meanwhile, I carry my own fears about not being good enough for them. My usual mask of strength and competence is thin today. Too thin.

Violet sits on top of the fort, drawing in her art book. I sit on the bench trying to look normal, whatever that means.

And then I see him.

Jace.

He's walking toward us with Harry, and I don't have time to rebuild my mask. I don't have the energy to pretend I'm fine.

He gives me that soft, careful smile he always gives me — the one that makes my stomach do something inconvenient.

I manage a small, tired smile back.

"Hi, Jace." My voice sounds thin. Not unfriendly — just worn.

He looks surprised. Like he wasn't expecting me to talk first.

"How's Harry doing today?" I ask, because it's safe.

"Good," he says. "He's good."

He laughs softly. "I think the group park play created a monster. This is our second trip here this week and he still wanted to come back."

I huff a quiet laugh.

He sits beside me while Harry runs to the slide.

I feel uncomfortable. This is not the day to expand my social circle.

Thankfully, Violet climbs down from the fort. She shows Jace her drawings, and he tells her how amazing they are.

I smile, but I need to leave. If I stay, I'll crack open. And I can't fall apart in front of him.

Not him.

"Violet, how about we make lasagne tonight?"

Her face lights up.

"We'll have to get the ingredients now before Archie's bus comes in," I say, edging away. "See you, Jace."

"Bye Mr Parker! Bye Harry!" Violet calls as she follows me.

Behind me, I can feel him watching.

I don't want to think about him. I know where my mind wants to go. It's not going there.

I have too much else to focus on.

And maybe that's for the best.

Chapter Twenty-Two

Finding Identity and Peace

Healing doesn't start when life gets easier. It starts when you finally give yourself permission to stop pretending you're fine.

Mickey's Blog Bits

Jace

"Anna says she's shy," Liam's words echo in my head as I watch Kayla and Violet walk away. Every nerve feels raw when she's around. Like she's sunlight and I'm not built for it.

Maybe I do need therapy.

Harry's happy doing laps on the slide with Banana, so I take out my phone and look up the blogs Mickey suggested. The first one catches my eye.

When life feels like you're trapped in a soap opera —finding the right support.

I click on it and start reading.

My Autistic Journey — Mickey

When life feels like you're trapped in a soap opera — finding the right support is crucial.

Anyone who knows me will tell you I don't like drama. But in my life, drama has always seemed to like me. Without going into too much detail, I had a traumatic childhood — the kind you don't realise is traumatic until you're older and someone finally gives you the language for it. A narcissistic parent. A series of events that forced me to grow up too fast. By my teens I was depressed, and I tried to end my life. Not long after, my sister was diagnosed with terminal cancer.

By adulthood, I was struggling. I started therapy to work through the trauma. Much later, I would be diagnosed as autistic and ADHD, and suddenly so many things made sense. But even before I had the words for who I was, therapy helped me in ways I'll never regret. Let me tell you some of the stories.

Jace

I pause halfway through the post, scrolling back up and skimming the sidebar.

There are dozens of entries — short ones, long ones, some barely a paragraph.

I don't read everything. I just click through the ones that feel closest to what I'm dealing with — the ones about burnout, anxiety, losing yourself, starting over. The ones that sound like me.

Then I go back to the next story.

Not Everyone Will Listen — Mickey

I've had therapy that changed my life — like the psychologist who used exposure therapy to help me overcome social anxiety. Each week was a tiny stretch outside my comfort zone. Eventually, I realised I'd done something I once thought impossible: I'd made friends.

But not every therapist is the right fit. I wrote this in a journal after one of the bad ones.

Another year, another counsellor's office. This time my workplace strongly recommended it. I was "too emotional," and students had walked in on me crying after hours. I kept it together while teaching, but when the room was empty, everything I'd been holding in would break through.

Each session was the same. I'd explain a situation where someone hurt me — like the time I was pulled into a room after church with two male youth leaders and the youth pastor. They told me the others had a problem with how "serious" I was. Then they told me to change or leave, with a heavy emphasis on leave. They already had my replacement waiting outside. No warning. No discussion. No support.

So I told her my stories. I shared the pain I never shared with anyone else. And then I wondered if I could share the biggest thing of all.

"Mickey, you've completed six sessions now," she said kindly. "I think you should talk to your doctor about medication. You've worked through these situations, and talking about them further won't change anything. Is there anything else you want to discuss today?"

My heart was pounding. I twisted my fingers in my lap. I took a breath and said the only word I had:
"I feel oppressed."

She snapped back instantly, authoritative and dismissive: "No one is oppressing you."

I shut down. Answered her questions with the shortest words possible.

Left the session knowing two things:

1. I would ask my doctor about medication because I couldn't keep crying like this.

2. I never wanted to speak to her again.

I had chosen the only word I could find to describe how I felt, and she shut it down.

It would take another decade before I understood what I'd been trying to say.

I wasn't oppressed by others — I was oppressing myself, shaped by childhood trauma and a mother who taught me to silence my own needs.

It was another counsellor, through schema therapy, who finally helped me understand and break free.

You can read more about that therapy — and the exposure therapy — in my other posts.

But let me leave you with this: Your life may feel like a soap opera, but the right therapist helps you rewrite the script.

Jace

I read slowly, absorbing every word, keeping one eye on Harry as he climbs the slide ladder for the fiftieth time.

It's not a judgement. Her saying I need therapy... it's not a judgement. It's just the truth.

And somehow, coming from her, it doesn't feel like failure. It feels like... permission.

I check on Harry again, then pull out my phone before I can talk myself out of it.

J: *Thank you. I'm going to try therapy.*

I hit send.

For the first time in a long time, it feels like I'm moving forward.

Chapter Twenty-Three

The First Session

My family was always opposed to therapy. For years I told myself it was just their generation, just their way. But the truth is, my life would have been so different if they'd sought help — and if I'd known I was allowed to seek it too.

Mickey's Blog Bits

Jace

The waiting room is too quiet. Too clean. Too still.

I bounce my knee, trying not to look like I'm about to bolt.

Harry's little dinosaur sticker is still stuck to my shirt from this morning. I didn't take it off. Felt wrong to.

The door opens.

"Jace?" the therapist says.

He's older than I expected. Calm face. Warm eyes. Steady presence.

I stand too fast. "Yeah. That's me."

His office is warm. Neutral. Nothing harsh.

I sit on the couch because the chair looks like it'll squeak if I breathe wrong.

He settles into his seat.

“So,” he says gently, “how can I help you today?”

My mouth is dry. I swallow.

“Your reviews said you help with... life changes. Anxiety. Depression.”

I rub my palms on my jeans. “That’s... kinda what I’m going through.”

He nods. “Tell me about that.”

And something in me just... breaks open. Not loud. Not dramatic. Just a slow, unstoppable spill.

“I lost hockey,” I say. “And that was... everything. My whole life. My identity. My future. I trained for a decade — longer — and then it was just gone. And I don’t know who I am without it.”

He doesn’t interrupt.

“And then I came here to help Liam, and I thought maybe I’d be useful, you know? But half the time I feel like I’m screwing everything up. Harry’s amazing, but he’s... a lot. And I’m trying, I swear I’m trying, but I don’t know what I’m doing.”

My voice cracks. I look away.

“And Liam’s doing better now. His wife Anna’s back. They’re happy. And I’m just... this extra guy on the couch taking up space.”

I exhale. “I go to this parent group with them. I like the people but... do I belong there?”

Still no judgement. Just listening.

“And then there’s the job offer.”

I laugh, but it’s not funny. “Seattle. Coaching. A real future. Something I should be excited about. But I’m not. I don’t feel anything. Or I feel too much. I can’t tell.”

He nods again, slow and steady.

“And Mel...”

I rub my face. "I feel like a jerk even saying this. She loved me. Would've given everything up for us. And when I realised I couldn't give her the one thing she really wanted, I also realised I didn't love her. I thought about her moving on and finding someone else and it didn't bother me at all. What kind of jackass, spends four years with someone without even realising he never loved them? I ended it so she wouldn't throw her life away on me. I had to be blunt with her recently cause she wouldn't give up on us and I still feel guilty."

I shake my head.

"The truth is... I realised I loved the idea of us or idea of companionship — not her. I wouldn't have given up everything for her and that makes me feel shallow. Like something's wrong with me."

He tilts his head. "Do you believe everyone should return affection just because it's given? Or at the same level it's given?"

I blink. "I... I don't know. I guess I thought I should."

"Why?"

I shrug helplessly. "Because it was a serious relationship and it feels like failing someone."

He lets that sit.

Then: "Is it just because this was a serious relationship or is this your view of all your relationships, friendships included?

I frown, " I guess all of them. Isn't that what relationships are supposed to be?"

"My question might seem strange. I'm trying to understand how you view relationships because it may be important later. It appears you are very demanding on yourself when it comes to relationships. Please continue."

I don't know what to do with that.

My thoughts jump again.

"And Kayla..."

I exhale hard. "I don't know what's going on there. She's..."

I trail off, stuck.

He waits, then says gently, "You brought Kayla up immediately after Mel. Do you feel like the same thing is happening here?"

“No.”

It’s out before I can think. “No. It’s not that. I just—”

I wince, trying to find the words.

“I have strong... responses? to her. And I feel stupid even saying that because she barely looks at me half the time. And when she does, I can’t tell if she’s being polite or if she actually—”

I stop myself. Shake my head.

“Doesn’t matter.”

He doesn’t push.

“And I’m alone here,” I say quietly. “New country. New everything. No team. No routine. No... me.”

The room is silent for a while.

Then he says, “You’ve been carrying a lot. For a long time.”

I nod, throat tight.

“You mentioned you were a professional hockey player. Have you been trying to handle it the same way you did your hockey career?" he asks.

I look at him perplexed, "What do you mean?

Athletes generally approach life with lots of discipline and hard work? They live by the moto work harder and it will solve itself?”

I look up.

He’s right. “That does sound like me. How did you know?”

“I have worked with a few athletes,” He says with a smile, “I understand professional sport.”

He continues, “But life isn’t the ice. You can’t train your way out of grief. Or identity loss. Or loneliness.”

That hits harder than I expect.

He leans forward slightly. “Let’s start simple. The job offer — Seattle. I want you to write a pros and cons list. Not what you think you *should* feel. What you actually feel.”

I nod slowly.

"Until I see you again, keep doing things you enjoy and be around people as much as you feel comfortable. And next session," he says, "we'll talk about the version of you that existed before hockey... and the version that can exist after."

I swallow hard.

"Okay."

When I leave the office, I feel lighter. Not fixed. Not healed. Just... lighter.

Raw, but lighter.

Like someone finally opened a window in a room I didn't realise I'd been suffocating in.

Chapter Twenty-Four

The Aftershock

Sometimes the hardest part of healing is going back to the places where you used to hide your pain — and realising you don't have to hide anymore

Mickey's Blog Bits

Jace

I go to the parent group on my therapist's advice to be around people, but I still feel strange being here. Like I'm wearing someone else's shoes.

I look over the job offer again while I wait for everyone to arrive. Forty days to decide. Forty. That's unheard of.

It should boost my mood, but it doesn't.

Liam and Anna are deep in conversation about Harry's assessment — they managed to get a cancellation appointment with the first stage of the assessment being next week. Good news. Big news. I'm happy for them. I am.

But I still feel... separate.

The door opens.

Kayla walks in with Janette.

I expect to be ignored, so I focus on my phone.

Someone sits beside me, and I put my phone away out of politeness.

Then I see who it is.

Kayla.

My breath falters.

Get it together, man. You're acting like a boy who's never seen a girl before. Deep breath.

"Howdy, Kayla. How was the lasagne the other night?" I drawl.

Smooth. Yep. Smooth.

She smiles. "Very good. Violet is becoming a great cook."

Her smile hits me like a punch. Holy hell, I'm acting like a smitten teddy bear.

"How long did it take to get Harry off the slide?" she chuckles.

"Not too long this time. He knew dinner was ready at home."

We both laugh.

"Anna said you used to play ice hockey professionally," she says.

"Yeah, I was on a pretty small team," I say, trying to downplay it.

"He was Captain when he got injured," Anna adds from the side.

She's proud. I can hear it. But I don't want to dwell on it.

Somehow Kayla senses that.

"Anna's been fortunate to have you around with Harry," she says, shifting the topic gently.

Harry runs up with his toy banana. "On kah Jay! Oo! Mee! Yoo! Ai!"

"He's been asking for you to take him on the ice for a week now," Liam says. "Ever since he saw footage of you playing."

Next to me, Kayla smiles — looking between me and Harry like she's seeing something she hadn't expected.

Then Priya calls her over.

She isn't avoiding me.

And that stupid little fact makes me happier than I've been in a while.

At the end of the meeting, as we're leaving, I hear Liam invite Kayla and her kids over for a game night.

I hold my breath.

She hesitates — just a flicker — then bows her head slightly, smiles, and looks up again.

"Sure," she says.

And something warm settles in my chest.

Maybe this is something for the con column.

But I quickly dismiss such foolishness.

Chapter Twenty-Five

Ice Healing

Sometimes joy doesn't return with fireworks. Sometimes it sneaks back in quietly, disguised as a moment you didn't plan — a laugh, a spark, a feeling you thought you'd lost for good.

Mickey's Blog Bits

Jace

Harry is vibrating.

Not bouncing. Not excited. Vibrating.

He's clutching his toy banana like it's a VIP guest and practically dragging me toward the rink doors.

"On kuh Jay! Iz! Izi! Iz!"

"Alright, buddy, slow down," I laugh, even though I'm grinning like an idiot. "Ice isn't going anywhere."

He doesn't slow down.

Inside, the cold hits us and Harry gasps like he's stepped into Narnia. *Something twists in my gut — quick, sharp — but I push it down. This is for Harry.*

I lace up his tiny skates — blue ones, because of course — and he wiggles his feet like he's already skating in his mind.

"You ready?" I ask.

He nods so hard his helmet shifts sideways.

We step onto the ice.

And he just... goes.

Not gracefully. Not coordinated. But fearless.

He slides, wobbles, flaps his arms, giggles, and somehow stays upright.

"Look at you!" I call out.

He beams. "Mee Iz boh!"

I swear my heart does something stupid.

I skate beside him, holding his hands at first, then letting go when he finds his rhythm. He copies everything I do — the little turns, the tiny hops, the glides. He's not good, not yet, but he's trying, and he's loving it.

And I'm loving it.

For the first time in... I don't even know how long...

I forget everything.

The job offer. The pressure. The loneliness. The confusion. The ache of losing hockey.

All of it melts away.

It's just me and Harry. Laughing. Skating. Existing.

And it feels good.

Really good.

After an hour, we come off the ice for lunch. Harry is still buzzing, cheeks pink, hair sweaty under his helmet.

Anna meets us at the café tables.

“Well?” she asks, smiling at Harry’s glow.

“He’s a natural,” I say, ruffling his hair. “Fearless little dude.”

Harry holds up his banana like it deserves credit.

Anna laughs. “There aren’t many programs he can do, you know. Not ones that fit him. And there’s nothing ice-related here for him.”

I nod, sipping my drink.

She continues, “A friend of Liam’s visited last year — she told us about Colorado. They have specialised sports programs for kids with disabilities. Especially winter sports. She said it was incredible. And Kayla said she took Archie and Violet there a couple of years ago and they were able to have adapted ski lessons at Winter Park.”

I look at Harry, who is currently making his banana ‘skate’ across the table.

Something warm flickers in my chest.

Anna goes on, “If Harry keeps responding like this… I’d love to take him there one day. Just to see what he could do.”

I don’t say anything.

But something shifts inside me.

A quiet click. A tiny spark. A feeling I haven’t felt in a long time.

Purpose.

I don’t know what it means yet. I don’t know where it leads. I don’t know if it changes anything.

But I know this:

Watching Harry on the ice felt right. Teaching him felt right. Being here felt right.

And for the first time since everything fell apart…

I don't feel lost.

Not completely.

Chapter Twenty-Six

Crossed Wires

It's wild how quickly we decide what someone else needs from us, then exhaust ourselves trying to deliver it... only to realise we never actually checked if that's what they wanted at all.

Mickey's Blog Bits

Jace

The high from skating with Harry is still buzzing under my skin when we get back to the house.

He's chattering to Anna about "ice jumps" and "banana spins," and she's smiling like her whole world is right there in front of her.

Liam steps out of the kitchen, wiping his hands on a towel. He looks tired — more tired than he lets on — but he still gives Harry a big grin.

"Good session?" he asks.

"Great," I say. "He loved it."

They both smile — proud, relieved, hopeful.

And somehow... that makes something twist in my chest.

Because they look like a family that's doing just fine. Better than fine. Solid. Stable. Together.

Like they don't need me anymore.

I clear my throat. "Hey, uh... I've been offered a coaching job in Seattle. I'm still thinking about it."

Anna's smile softens. "Of course. That's an incredible opportunity."

Liam nods quickly — too quickly. "Yeah, man. You should take it seriously. Don't worry about us."

Something in the way he says it makes me pause.

"Right," I say. "I just... didn't want to leave you guys in the lurch, but you seem good now."

Anna shakes her head immediately. "It's amazing having you here, but we'll be okay."

But her eyes flicker — just for a second — with something she doesn't want me to see.

Liam adds, "We've got systems now. Routines. And Anna's back. I'm working on being more supportive. Things are... good."

He says it with a smile, but his shoulders sag a little.

He's exhausted. They both are. And they're hiding it.

For me.

Maybe they don't want to be the reason I stay. Maybe I'm just trying to convince myself they need me.

I swallow. "Yeah. Okay."

Harry runs up and grabs my hand. "Jay! Iz 'gain mo-wo?"

Before I can answer, Anna gently redirects him. "We'll see, sweetheart. Uncle Jace has a lot going on, and I thought we were having a banana morning tea."

A lot going on. Right.

I force a smile. "You enjoy the banana morning tea. Maybe we can go another time, buddy."

Harry beams, completely unaware of the shift in the room. "Na na tee and Iz!"

Liam claps my shoulder. "Seriously, man. Don't stay here on our account. You've already done more than enough."

More than enough.

I know he means thank you. But all I hear is:

We don't need you anymore.

Anna gives me a warm smile — too warm, too careful. "We just want you to be happy, Jace."

I nod, because I can't trust my voice.

I know I need to give them their space. I need to find my own path and let them have theirs.

So why do I feel guilty for not telling them the truth? Guilt for letting them think I'm hesitating because of them. Guilt for wanting to stay.

As I head to my room, I hear Harry call after me, "On kuh Jay! Iz boh!"

His little voice hits me harder than anything else.

I close my door quietly.

The buzz from the ice fades. And the weight of the decision settles heavier than ever.

Chapter Twenty-Seven

Game Night

Have you ever met someone you're so in tune with that they should absolutely be your best friend — but opening yourself up to that possibility feels like handing your fragile little heart to someone and hoping they don't drop it? Sometimes the connection is obvious... but letting yourself lean into it is the terrifying part.

Mickey's Blog Bits

Jace

Archie and Harry are settled in the lounge room with the Mario Bros movie playing on the TV and a table full of snacks. They're already sticky-fingered and happy, which buys us at least twenty minutes of peace.

Liam calls the rest of us into the attached dining area.

"Okay," he says, clapping his hands. "Teams are me and Anna, Violet and Aleia, and Jace and Kayla."

He pairs us up on purpose. I know he does. He knows he does. Anna definitely knows he does. Kayla... probably knows too.

But she still sits beside me at the table, pulling her chair closer to mine and away from Violet with a grin.

"Just creating some distance so you don't cheat off me," she teases Violet.

I huff a laugh.

“I can't cheat, it’ll be obvious." Violet protests." I'm terrible at hiding things,”

Her eyes flicker — amused, warm — and something in my chest loosens.

“Mum,” Violet warns, “you’re going down.”

Kayla turns to me, eyes bright. “You better have your A game ready, JP. We have to wipe the table with these wannabes.”

She used my hockey nickname.

I don’t know whether to be shocked... or thrilled.

“Yes, boss,” I say, leaning back with a grin. “Fixin’ to win this whole rodeo.”

The atmosphere crackles — smiles, sass, taunts flying everywhere.

“Alright, y’all,” Liam says, rubbing his hands together. “Anna suggested we start with Cranium since it has the greatest variety.”

Kayla leans in, whispering, “Prepare to be amazed.”

I already am.

The Sculpting Round

Kayla draws the first card — sculpting — reads it silently, and groans.

“Oh no. No, absolutely not.”

“What?” I ask.

She hides the card. “I can’t show you. You have to guess.”

She mutters, “I can’t believe I have to do this with Play-Doh,” but she starts sculpting anyway.

And somehow, without talking, I know exactly what she’s building.

She shapes the base. Adds the cockpit. Adds the dish.

I name each part as she forms it, and she looks up at me with this spark — like she's surprised and delighted at the same time.

"Millennium Falcon," I announce.

Everyone else cranes their necks to see.

Violet groans. "Ugh, they're going to win."

The game continues around the circle with everyone winning their round.

The Wordplay Round

Kayla reads the next card — a wordplay card — silently, eyes widening. "Oh boy."

"What is it?" I ask.

She shakes her head. "Just... try. Spell *anachronistic* backwards."

I inhale, already nervous.

Her eyes are huge, willing me to get it right.

Slowly, I spell out, "C I T S I N O R H C A N A."

Kayla face lights up.

Anna stares. "Are you two communicating telepathically?"

Aleia's jaw drops. "No. Absolutely not. That's witchcraft."

Kayla looks at me, stunned. "How did you—?"

I shrug, trying to play it cool. "You gave me the answer with your eyebrows."

Her cheeks flush. Mine probably do too.

Once again everyone wins their next round.

The Trivia Round

I draw the next card, read it silently, and grin.

“What actor has appeared in both Star Wars and Marvel as a female lead?”

Kayla doesn’t even blink. “Natalie Portman.”

Liam throws his hands up. “No. I refuse. You two are cheating.”

“We’re not,” Kayla says, flustered. “We’re just—”

“Sharing one brain,” Violet mutters.

Kayla goes pink.

I pretend not to notice... but I’m loving it.

Kayla

I can't believe how in sync we are.

The next round goes well for everyone else, and Liam suggests a quick break — Harry needs to go to bed, and Archie has fallen asleep on the couch. Violet and Aleia huddle together, whispering strategy like they're planning a coup.

"It don't matter what you do," Jace taunts them, slipping into a drawl and tipping an imaginary cowboy hat. "We're gonna whoop your ar— butt."

I laugh. "I think all those questions were ideal for me. I love Star Wars and Marvel."

He looks at me with a smile that almost stops my breath. "I love them too. What's your favourite Star Wars trilogy?"

"The first one — episodes four, five, and six."

His eyes light up. "Same."

And then it happens — the rapid-fire questions, the answers flying back and forth so fast I can't remember who asked what.

Favourite Marvel movie? Too many / Iron Man or No Way Home.

Favourite food? Pizza / Fried chicken and biscuits.

Favourite sport? Basketball / Hockey, duh.

Favourite genre? Sci-fi / Sci-fi.

Favourite movie? Shawshank / Agreed.

We go through everything — Harry Potter, Lord of the Rings, Stargate, Star Trek, Andromeda, Firefly, Jurassic Park.

We even agree that, much as we love the originals, Twisters and Top Gun: Maverick were surprisingly better.

I'm having so much fun.

Why had I avoided him?

he Humming Round

The game continues for five more rounds.

If we win this next question, Jace and I win the whole thing.

I pick up the card — a humming challenge.

Everyone can play.

My heart is pounding.

If our conversation was anything to go by... we've got this.

I look up at Jace and give him a smile.

Then I hum four notes. "Ah, ah. Ah, ah." I hum them like I'm auditioning for the Star Wars soundtrack.

Just four

"Duel of the Fates!" he shouts.

I stare at him like he just read my soul. He can't be this perfect.

"That was barely a sound," Anna groans.

"It was enough," he says, grinning. "You hum like someone who knows the Force personally."

I laugh — bright, unguarded, real.

Protests erupt around the room.

"Bless your heart," he says, slipping into a heavy Texan drawl. "Y'all didn't think you'd win, did ya?"

I laugh even harder.

The mood is electric.

The Group Cards

We decide to keep playing cards as a group while we share a cuppa before heading home.

Violet hums the Simpsons theme; Aleia screams the answer.

Liam sculpts the Leaning Tower of Pisa; Anna gets it instantly and whines, "Where were these cards before?"

Archie wakes up and wanders over to join us.

Jace draws a charades card: act out a famous movie object.

He squats, cups his hands in front of him, widens his eyes and puts on creepy expression, staring at his hands and mouthing 'My precious'.

I scream out "My precious," in my best Gollum voice. Then to mess with him I call out Samwise Gamgee with a huge teasing smile on my face.

"Kayla, you're killin' me," he gasps dramatically, clutching his chest.

Everyone bursts out laughing — loud, bright, unfiltered.

Then Archie demands, "Mum sing."

So I hum the Star Wars theme — a bit off key.

Archie squeals.

Violet and Aleia join in.

Anna laughs so hard she hides her face in Liam's chest.

Jace just smiles at me.

I haven't had this much fun in a long time.

If it wasn't so late, I'd stay here till morning.

But I have to get Aleia home, so I say my goodbyes.

I want to say something to Jace, but suddenly I feel awkward.

"Thanks for the help to win, JP. Until next time we slaughter them."

Everyone groans as the kids push me toward the door.

"No way you two are on the same team next time," Liam teases.

Chapter Twenty-Eight

Infatuation and the Fear Beneath

There's a special kind of fear that comes with wanting something good. Not because you doubt the thing itself, but because you doubt your ability to hold it without breaking it — or yourself.

Mickey's Blog Bits

Kayla

Jane chooses the café — she always does — a quiet place tucked behind a bookshop, all warm wood and mismatched mugs. Just the right mix of chic yet eclectic style, just like Jane. It smells like cinnamon and old paper. It feels safe.

She's already there when I arrive, waving me over with that soft, knowing smile that makes me feel completely at ease, even though my mask has never fooled her. She sees through it even when I don't realise I'm wearing it.

"Hey, stranger," she says, standing to hug me. "You look tired."

"I have kids," I deadpan.

She snorts. "So do I. That's not what I meant."

Of course it isn't.

We sit. She talks first — she always does — telling me about her boys. One with autism, one with ADHD and anxiety. The chaos. The joy. The exhaustion. The constant adjusting. The constant learning. Then about everything to do with her husband. All three are redheads.

There are so many things I like about Jane, including her love of red hair. I joke with her often that her husband has nothing to fear from other men — unless they're ginger. I continue to listen. I love hearing about them. It's grounding.

But she's watching me too closely.

"So," she says lightly, stirring her tea, "how are you?"

I give her the script.

The polished, acceptable version of my life.

"Work's busy. The kids are good. Violet's thriving with her new routine. Archie's... Archie. I'm fine."

Jane's eyebrows lift.

"Kayla," she says gently, "that was the most scripted answer I've heard from you in years. Do you want to talk about what you're avoiding?"

I look away. "No and yes. This isn't a therapy session, Jane."

"No," she agrees. "It's a friend who can see something is eating you and is offering to listen. And I'm not going to push. I'm not going to analyse you. I'm just going to listen unless you ask me to do something else."

Her voice is warm. Steady. Safe.

And suddenly I feel like I'm standing on the edge of something I don't want to name.

I pick at the sleeve of my jumper. "It's stupid."

"Most fears feel stupid until you say them out loud."

I swallow.

"It's... it's the limerence again."

She looks confused, "Limerence?"

I forget that I get attached to certain old-fashioned words.

"I mentioned it before. You know – the sudden involuntary, intense obsession with another person, that is connected to intrusive thoughts, and a longing for returned attention or affection," I explain reciting the almost dictionary-perfect definition I've given therapists before.

Her eyes soften instantly. "Ah. Infatuation. Who? New friend?"

I'm silent. Staring at the table. It feels like forever.

I feel Jane's gaze sharpen. "It's a romantic interest?"

My head snaps up — and instead of judgement, she has unshed tears in her eyes and a huge smile on her face.

"This is awesome," she says.

I shake my head. "No. No it's not. You know me. You know my extremes. I can't control my brain. I dive in too fast and I give too much. And then it falls apart and I break."

"I don't know how to do this," I whisper. "I don't know how to take things slow. I never have. I'm either all in or not at all. And when I fall—"

"You fall hard," she finishes.

I nod.

"And you're terrified."

Another nod.

"Of being crushed."

My throat tightens. "Yes."

Jane doesn't say anything. She just waits. Present. Patient.

"I haven't felt this in years," I admit. "Not since before the kids. And I don't trust it. I don't trust myself with it. I don't trust what it does to me."

"I've avoided any relationship that brought up intense emotions for a decade. This is how I protect myself and my family. I'm not made like everyone else."

The words spill out like a defence I've rehearsed for years.

She remains silent, just listening.

"You think I'm overreacting, don't you?"

"I would never say overreacting," she says softly. "But you are making a choice that could be self-sabotaging. And you're struggling to even intellectualise the way you normally do. Which tells me that maybe you're ready to confront this."

She winces a bit, aware she just skirted the line between counsellor and friend.

“Do you want me to continue?” she asks.

I nod.

Jane’s expression is so full of warmth it almost hurts.

“You’ve been through so much that you’ve learned to avoid any big emotions you can't control,” she says. “But the way you grasp control is by avoiding anything that feels uncertain. The problem is you're denying yourself the chance of the good things too. You're staying on the shore instead of risking the waves."

“Avoidance feels safer,” she adds with a kind smile.

“Yes,” I breathe. “So much safer.”

“But it’s not working anymore, Kayla.”

I close my eyes. “No.”

“Because you’ve found someone who isn’t just attractive,” she says gently. “He’s compatible.”

The words hit me like a physical thing.

I don’t deny it.

I can’t.

Jane reaches across the table and squeezes my hand. “Kayla... wanting connection isn’t a flaw. Being afraid of it isn’t either. But you’re allowed to want something good. You’re allowed to take a chance.”

“I don’t know how,” I whisper.

“You don’t have to know how,” she says. “You just have to stop running from the fact that you want to.”

I stare at her, heart pounding.

Because she’s right.

Avoiding him isn’t protecting me anymore. It’s hurting me.

“And Kayla,” she adds softly, “in the time I’ve known you, you’ve set stronger boundaries. You’ve reduced your fawning. You’ve built a solid identity and real self-confidence. You are not the same woman who put these walls up before you had the kids.”

That finally breaks me. The tears fall.

She's right.

I'm stronger now.

I can't keep living like this.

Avoidance is keeping me stuck in a life smaller than the one I want.

And for the first time, I let myself feel it fully:

I want him. I want the way he laughs with me. The way he listens. The way he sees me. The way we fit.

And wanting him terrifies me.

But pretending I don't want him?

That's starting to terrify me more.

"I'm sorry for spilling all this on you. We were meant to be catching up," I say, wiping my tears.

"Oh hush," Jane says, shaking her head with a smile. "This is friendship, Kayla. With how rarely you share your pain with me, there is no way you're overburdening anything."

The conversation drifts again to her husband and the boys.

We spend the rest of the afternoon laughing and catching up.

But the truth sits warm and heavy in my chest.

Maybe I'm ready to stop running from my feelings.

Chapter Twenty-Nine

Attention to Values

Sometimes the hardest part isn't choosing between two paths — it's admitting which one you actually want. Especially when the thing you want isn't a job or a plan, but a person, something you can't control and wouldn't want to.

Mickey's Blog Bits

Jace

I clutch the worksheet Mark asked me to complete between sessions as he gestures for me to sit. I hand him the paper like a kid, turning in an assignment he already knows is wrong. "It's the pros and cons list," I say. "For the coaching job."

Pros	Cons
Great Money	It's not the career I wanted
It's in America - no visa issue	I only became a coach because it was hockey adjacent
Its hockey - so familiar	I was thinking of studying
I can protect other players	Or starting a new career
Safe choice	It feels like settling
It's a good step on a path	It feels like running

Kayla

He nods. "Let's take a look."

He scans the list. It's messy. My handwriting's terrible. But it's honest.

Taking the Coaching Job

Mark studies the page for a long moment. Then he sets it aside and pulls out a couple of sheets.

“You mentioned wanting to understand what matters most to you,” he says. “Would you be open to trying something called a Valued Living Questionnaire? It might help us see what’s underneath this list.”

I nod. “Sure.”

I fill it out, asking questions when I need to. When I’m done, he places the two lists side by side.

“What do you notice when you look at these?” he asks.

I stare at the categories.

“Relationships are important to me — family and personal — but I’ve only been giving attention to family. ... Friends matter to me, but I haven’t given them the same amount of effort. ... Work is one of the least important categories. ... Community is important, more than citizenship. I love America, but I don’t have to live there. It’s just... easier. ... I like learning new things, but I haven’t done much of that since I’ve been here — or I have, but not in a way that feels meaningful. ... Everything else seems... where it should be?”

I look up, unsure.

Mark nods slowly. “That’s a thoughtful reflection. When you compare that to your pros and cons list, what stands out to you?”

I shrug. “The pros are obvious. Money. Stability. Hockey. It’s what I know. And it’s all work related.”

He gestures gently toward the other column. “And the cons?”

I swallow. “The cons are... the things I value. Family. Community. Friends. Learning something new...”

He doesn’t speak — just waits.

And something in me keeps going.

“I feel like I can have those things here,” I say. “But if I had them there, they’d be... professional. Not personal. My family is here. And hockey season is eight or nine months of the year. The only friendships you can maintain are with the team, and even that’s hard with away games.”

Mark nods, letting me continue.

"I've been thinking about what life would actually look like if I took the job," I say. "It's not just the travel — it's the rhythm. You wake up, train, coach, travel, repeat. You live in locker rooms and airports. You talk about the game, you think about the game, you breathe the game. And that used to be enough. But now... it isn't."

He stays quiet, listening.

"I used to think hockey was everything," I say. "But lately, I've realised it's just the thing I know best. It's safe because it's familiar. But it's also the thing that keeps me from trying anything else. I could take the job and be fine — financially, professionally — but I'd still be stuck in the same loop. I'd still be the guy who never moved on."

Mark gives a small nod, encouraging me to keep going.

"I think I want something that feels like growth," I admit. "Something that doesn't just keep me busy. I want to learn again — not just drills or plays, but something new. I've been thinking about studying sports science or physio. Maybe finding work here. Something that still connects to what I love but lets me build something different."

He waits, still quiet.

"And community," I add. "That's the part that keeps coming up. There's a parent group I go to with my brother and his wife. They've become like friends. A community built on connection rather than profession. I've been visiting the ice rink here since I took Harry, and I'm making friends there too. I feel like I belong here. Not because of my work — because of me."

I take a breath. "My family is here. I'm happy being near them. But I need my own life, not theirs."

Mark nods once. "It sounds like you're starting to picture what that life could look like."

"Yeah," I say quietly. "It's not clear yet, but it feels... possible."

He glances at the page again. "Tell me about the name in the middle."

My whole body freezes.

He waits.

"I mentioned Kayla last time," I say.

He nods for me to continue.

"She doesn't fit in either column. She's not a pro or a con. She's... a reason. A reason to turn down the job. A reason to stay. A reason to figure out who I am now."

Mark stays quiet, giving me space.

"And that's the part that scares me," I admit. "Because I don't know what I'm doing. I don't know what I'd do if I stayed. Hockey is all I've ever known. If I don't take the job... what then? I can't live off my brother and his wife forever. They won't say it, but they don't need me anymore. Harry's doing better. They're finding their rhythm. And I'm just... there."

The words start tumbling out faster.

"And Kayla—God. I don't even know what I feel yet. I think I know. But I'm not sure. And even if I was sure, why would she want me? What do I have to offer? I don't have a career. I don't have a plan. I don't even know who I am without hockey. And then there's the injury. The infertility. The PTSD. All the things that make me... me. All the things I can't change."

My throat tightens.

"She already has kids. So maybe the infertility won't matter to her. But I don't even know if it matters to me. I always thought I'd probably be a dad. That's the plan isn't it, grow up, get married and have kids. I even considered starting a year back to make Mel happy, but then found out I couldn't because of the injury. And what if I'm not even good with kids? What if I mess them up?"

Mark's expression stays steady, grounded.

"And the PTSD..." I swallow hard. "I had counselling for it. Mel knew about it. She thought that's why we broke up. She said I never let her help me. And maybe she was right. Maybe I don't know how to let anyone in."

I drag a hand over my face. "And the accident... watching someone I was responsible for almost die... that doesn't go away. It's not nightmares. It's flashes. It's slowed down a lot. I can even skate now without it surfacing, but I don't know if that ever stops."

Mark lets the silence stretch.

Then, gently: "You unpacked a lot there, Jace. A lot of pain. A lot of fear. A lot of longing."

He pauses. "Would I be right in saying that most of what troubles you is fear of the unknown?"

I nod.

"Is there anything you said that is certain? Confirmed?"

I open my mouth, then close it again. The infertility — is that a fact, or just the fear of being less? I shake my head.

"So would I be right in saying that, with the exception of the PTSD and the things you're grieving — the loss of your career, your identity, and the infertility — most of what's worrying you is that your life is in limbo, and you're struggling with uncertainty."

I nod.

He taps the centre of the page. "You didn't write 'money.' You didn't write 'career.' You wrote a person. And when you spoke a moment ago, you only mentioned those things in relation to being useful or wanted by the people in your life. That's information. It tells me that beyond the grief, the trauma, and the uncertainty, what you really value — what you want — is connection. Belonging. To a community, to who you are beyond hockey, to your family, and to a romantic partner."

I let out a shaky breath. "Yeah. It tells me I'm screwed."

He gives a small, steady smile. "It tells me she matters."

I look down at my hands. "She does. And that's the problem. If she matters, then I can lose her. And I don't know if I can handle that."

Mark nods. "Let's slow this down. I'm not ignoring or diminishing how strongly you feel about Kayla. But with everything you've described today, it would be normal for your capacity to cope with setbacks to be reduced. One thing at a time."

He waits until I'm looking at him.

"Before I see you again, I want you to focus on building connections — with your family, with the people you've met here in Australia, and with the people you still have in America. If you get the chance to connect with Kayla, take it. But take it slowly. Give yourself space to heal in the other areas of your life."

He taps the notebook between us.

“We started these sessions because of the job and how you were feeling. If you’re willing, I want to help you start moving through the grief — the loss of what you knew, the identity you built around hockey — so you can become confident in what you want for your future.”

I understand what Mickey was saying, the right therapist really listens and can clarify with you what you actually need. I think for what seems like a long moment.

“I was thinking of looking at what alternative career options I might have in Perth.” I say quietly. “I also thought I might see what else I like doing other than hockey”

Mark nods once. “That will be really helpful. It will give you something to focus on outside of the loss”

“I know what you said but what if I find a life here I want and ...”

There is a significant pause as I study my hands. "Kayla is not a part of it," Mark finished for me.

I nod.

He considers that. “Let’s imagine both outcomes. If you find a career path here and Kayla isn’t interested... what then?”

I swallow. “I’d feel the way Mel felt when I couldn’t love her. And I think that would be devastating. But if I chose a career here, it would be because I want to do it, and not because she is here."

“Is that the worse-case scenario or is it worse if she is interested?”

I let out a breath that shakes. “Then I’d be terrified.”

“Why?”

“Because none of the things I’m scared of go away just because she wants me. The infertility. The PTSD. The uncertainty. The fear I’m not enough. The fear I’ll hurt her. Or disappoint her. Or not be what she needs. Or what her kids need. Wanting her doesn’t fix any of that.”

"And why do you fear all of that?" he asks.

I catch a look on Mark's face, like he knows I'm close to a crucial understanding and then I realise, "because it's the worse-case scenario in my head and none of it may ever happen. Everything is so uncertain, that I'm imagining everything could go wrong."

Mark smiles and nods slowly. "You've processed a lot today. And every part of it matters. We'll explore each of these—your identity after hockey, the grief of infertility, the trauma from the accident, the feelings of not being enough. There's no rush. We take it at your pace."

I nod.

He concludes, "As I said before, concentrate on building those connections and look for other career options. Everything else we can work on in therapy. You said you still had 25 days now to decide about the job. We have 3 sessions booked before you need to make a decision – you set the topics and the pace. I will follow your lead."

For the first time, I don't feel alone with the heavy feelings I've been trying to suppress. And for the first time, I feel a flicker of curiosity — maybe even hope—about what kind of future the City of Perth could offer.

Chapter Thirty

Connection Begins

There are moments when connection feels effortless — like slipping into a rhythm you didn't know you were capable of. And that ease can be just as terrifying as the fear that came before it.

Mickey's Blog Bits

Jace

It's Liam's week on site, and Anna texts the group chat that she'll be late — Harry's diagnostic assessment appointment ran long.

So when I walk into the community room, it's quieter than usual. Softer. Less chaotic.

Kayla's already there.

She's sitting at the table, flipping through the laminated visual schedule Angela made for the children in the group. Her hair is down, curls loose around her face, and she looks... calm. Peaceful. Beautiful.

She glances up when I walk in.

"Oh. Hey, JP."

My chest does something stupid.

"Hey," I say, trying to sound normal. "Mind if I sit?"

She gestures to the chair beside her. "Go for it."

I sit. Close enough to feel her warmth. Not close enough to scare her.

People trickle in — Priya, Angela, Tom, a couple of new parents — and the room breaks into smaller conversations. No big circle tonight. Just pockets of people talking.

Kayla and I end up in our own little pocket.

"I really enjoyed the quiz night," she says, tucking a curl behind her ear.

I smile. "Me too. It was amazing."

"I think we should definitely do more of them," she suggests.

"Yeah," I say. "Definitely. Or maybe a barbecue."

"Ooo, Australian barbecue or Texan barbecue?" she teases.

"Oh, one hundred percent Texan barbecue. I make a fantastic smoked brisket."

"Yum. Now I'm hungry."

Tom leans over. "Did someone say Texan barbecue? I hope I'm invited."

Suddenly everyone is talking about barbecue and whether they've ever had a real Texan one.

And this — this right here — is the community I want. Not because of Anna and Liam. Not because of Harry. Because I like these people. They're good people.

The conversations drift apart again, and I'm drawn back to Kayla.

"What about you?" I ask. "How's your week been?"

She laughs under her breath. "Chaotic. Violet's been hyper-focusing on Pokémon evolutions, and Archie has decided he only watches this new kids' singing show."

I grin. "They know what they want."

"True," she replies, smiling.

We talk.

About her work. About shared interests. About childhood dreams — hers to be a singer or to travel, mine full of ice rinks and early mornings. About parenting — the exhaustion, the joy, the guilt, the pride.

Even when it gets a bit awkward, it feels right. Like we're both trying not to lean too far in but failing anyway.

At one point she says something funny about Violet's literal interpretations of idioms, and I laugh too hard.

At another point I tell her about Harry's obsession with snails and how he keeps putting them in Anna's bowls, and she laughs too hard.

It feels... good. It feels like something beginning.

Eventually the group winds down. People pack up. Chairs scrape. Kids whine. Bags zip.

Kayla stands, slinging her tote over her shoulder.

"Well," she says, "I should get going. School pick-ups soon."

"Yeah," I say. "I should go too."

But I don't move.

Neither does she.

There's a moment — a soft, suspended moment — where the air feels charged and fragile at the same time.

My heart is pounding. My palms are sweating. I can hear Mark's voice in my head:

Longing isn't weakness. It's direction.

I take a breath.

"Kayla?"

She looks up at me, eyes wide, hopeful, scared.

"Yeah?"

I swallow. "Would you... like to go out sometime?"

Her breath catches. I see it — the fear, the instinct to run, and I start panicking too. What am I, twelve.

But then something else flickers across her face.

Courage.

She nods once, small but certain.

"Yes," she says quietly. "I'd like that."

And just like that, something begins.

And I remind myself: slow. Take it slow.

We settle on a day and time. She's about to leave when the door opens and Anna rushes in.

Kayla

My insides are doing cartwheels after Jace asked me out. I'm trying so hard to look calm that I excuse myself quickly — but when I turn, I stop dead.

Anna has just arrived.

But this isn't normal-late Anna. She wouldn't come at the end of group unless something was wrong.

I walk toward her slowly, ready to ask if she needs help.

"He's autistic, and they suspect ADHD," she blurts out.

I blink. "Harry?"

She nods, eyes wide and wet.

I feel Jace step up behind me, silent but steady.

"How are you feeling about it?" I ask softly.

"Relieved. Confused. Overwhelmed," she splutters. "I knew, but..."

I turn to Jace. "How about you take Harry home, and Anna and I can go have a coffee?"

Anna nods, grateful and shaky. Jace squeezes her shoulder and calls out to Harry.

As I guide Anna toward the door, I ask gently, "Have you called Liam yet?"

She shakes her head, tears spilling. "No. I... I didn't want to say it out loud until I saw someone who understood. He wanted to be there, but I think he was more anxious about the outcome than he admitted. We agreed I'd go, and we'd talk about it together afterwards."

I squeeze her hand.

"I'm right here."

And even with my heart still fluttering from Jace...this is where I need to be.

And I am grateful for the distraction, to stop my mind from spiraling a little longer.

Chapter Thirty-One

First Date: Navigating Thin Ice

> *People talk about vulnerability like it's a choice. But sometimes it's not. Sometimes your body tells the truth your mouth never would — and all you can do is hope the right person sees you and stays.*
>
> Mickey's Blog Bits

JACE

Since I brought Harry to the rink, I have been here regularly, just to skate laps and shut out all the external noise and pressure. Each time the cold air hits my face, something in me settles. Ice has always been the one place that brought me joy.

No noise. No pressure. Just movement.

God, I missed this.

The clean air. The echo. The bite of the ice.

My home.

I'm halfway down memory lane before I realise Kayla isn't beside me. She's walking slowly behind, hands tucked into her sleeves, eyes darting around like she's checking for exits.

But that's nothing new. She always looks like she's planning escape routes. Maybe she's anxious. Maybe she's just shy. It's only our first date — I'm not reading into it.

"You ever skated before?" I ask.

She hesitates. A tiny pause.

“Once,” she says. “Not very successfully.”

There's a flicker of something in her voice. Fear, maybe. Nervousness.

I tell myself it's just first-date jitters.

“Perfect,” I grin. “I'll show you how.”

And yeah, my mind wanders — the way she will fit against me when I steady her, the way she might smile if she gets it right. I’m embarrassingly proud of myself for the date idea. I know it’s obnoxious, but I’ve never really had to try before... and I’ve never wanted to impress someone this badly.

She nods, but her shoulders are tight. First dates are weird. And I’m rusty at this too.

We lace up on the bench. I’m done in seconds — muscle memory — and she’s still working on her laces, fingers slow and careful. I don’t think much of it. Not everyone grew up on skates.

Something in her posture tugs at me — too still, too careful — but I brush it off as nerves.

“Ready?” I ask.

She nods again, same tight shoulders.

I step onto the ice first, letting the glide take me.

God, it feels good.

I push off, skate a lazy loop, then another. When I turn back, she’s smiling at me from the gate — small, shy, but real. I show off a little. Some speed. A few tricks. Every time she laughs, I push it a little more. Her eyes on me feel... good.

After a while, I circle back. “Your turn,” I say, reaching for her hand.

“You go skate,” she says softly. “I’ll just come on slowly and get used to the ice.”

There’s fear in her eyes. I give her space. I don’t want to push.

When I loop around again, she’s still on the rubber mat, clutching the rail like it’s the only thing keeping her upright.

“Come on,” I say gently, moving toward her slowly. “I got you.”

KAYLA

I step onto the ice, gripping the rail with everything I have.

My brain screams.

My body freezes.

The ground tilts.

I try to move — just a little — but my skate slides further than I meant it to, and the rest of my body doesn't follow. My legs don't listen. My balance is gone. My heart slams against my ribs.

Then arms wrap around me.

Steady. Warm. Safe.

Relief floods me so fast I almost sag into him. I smile — small, shaky — because for a second, I think I can do this. He turns me gently, whispers encouragement, smiles like warm afternoon sun.

Then he takes my arms.

And pulls me away from the wall.

No no no no—

The movement is too fast. Too loose. Too uncontrolled.

My stomach drops. My vision tunnels. My breath shatters.

I grip him harder — too hard — but I can't stop.

I can't think. I can't breathe.

The ice shifts under me — or maybe I shift — and suddenly I'm falling.

I hit the ice.

Cold explodes through me.

Everything breaks.

I curl in on myself, knees to chest, hands over my head, rocking without meaning to.

Too much. Too fast. Too loud. Too bright.

My heartbeat pounds in my ears.

I want to disappear. I want to vanish into the ice. I want this to stop.

Too much movement. Too much everything.

I can't—No—No—

JACE

She's curled up on the ice, shaking, crying, rocking like she's trying to hold herself together.

"Kayla—Kayla—hey—hey—look at me—"

But she can't.

I've seen panic attacks before — teammates, fans, even my brother once — but this is different.

This is like she's not here at all.

People are staring.

I don't care.

I crouch beside her, hands up, not touching — I don't know if touch will help or make it worse.

"Kayla," I say softly. "I'm right here. You're okay. You're safe."

She doesn't respond. Doesn't look up. Doesn't even seem to hear me.

My chest twists.

And then —my body betrays me.

A flash. A sound. A memory.

The crack of my knee. The scream of metal on ice. Years later, another player hitting the ice and not getting back up. The sickening moment when you know you can't stop the impact. Different moment. Same helpless feeling.

My breath stutters. My vision narrows. My hands go cold.

I can't move.

I'm right here beside her, but my body is locked — frozen — like I'm thirty-three again, watching someone fall and knowing I can't undo it.

I surface from the flashback not knowing how much time has passed. Seconds, probably. The people around us haven't moved on yet.

Guilt slams into me so hard I almost choke on it.

I did this. I pushed her. I pulled her off the wall. I made her fall.

My fault. My fault. My fault.

I try to reach for her — my hand won't move.

I try to speak — my throat closes.

I'm useless. I'm still not fully grounded from the flashback. I'm failing her.

Minutes pass. We stay there like we are frozen in time. Some people start to offer help. Most stare. A few glare like she's ruining their fun.

I force myself — literally force my muscles — to move. To breathe. To be here.

Slowly, I reach out and stroke her back. She doesn't pull away — doesn't react at all — but after a moment, her breaths start to even out. She turns her face toward my hand, then her body, sliding an inch across the ice until she's leaning into my chest.

She's still sobbing, but softer now. Smaller.

"Help me off the ice, please," she whispers.

KAYLA

Jace wraps his arms around me tighter. Warm. Steady. Safe.

But I'm too mortified to feel any of it.

He pulls back and signals to someone. Another man comes, and together they help me up and across to the gate. My legs barely work. They steady me as I step off the ice.

The moment my skates hit the mat, I drop onto the nearest bench and tear at the laces with shaking hands. I mumble something about needing the bathroom and bolt.

Inside the ladies' room, I find a cubicle, close the lid, lock the door, and sit.

And I cry.

Hard.

There is no way he'll want to see me again.

He loves the ice — I saw it in the way he came alive out there.

And I ruined it.

I ruined everything.

Why did I ever think I could do this? Why did I think I could date? Why did I think I could be normal?

I bury my face in my hands and sob until my chest aches.

I just want to go home. Lock myself in my room. Disappear.

Chapter Thirty-Two

Aftermath

It's wild how quickly we assume we've ruined everything, even when the other person is still standing right there. Shame makes us forget that connection isn't fragile — it's tested.

Mickey's Blog Bits

Kayla

When I finally emerge from the bathroom, Jace is waiting. I couldn't look at him properly. Just asked if he could take me home. The trip home was silent but he tried and I tried to give something, anything back.

By the time I get home, I'm already shaking.

I make it to my room, close the door, and sit on the edge of the bed, drained, with my phone in my hand.

I stare at it for a long time before finally pressing call.

Jane answers on the first ring.

"Well?" she demands. "Tell me everything. How was the date?"

I try to speak.

What comes out is a broken laugh.

"It was a disaster," I whisper. "I ruined it. I always ruin it."

"Oh boy," Jane mutters. "Start talking."

I give her the summary — the rink, the fall, the panic, the crying, the bathroom, the shame.

Every word makes my chest tighten.

"He was so apologetic," I say, voice cracking. "And it was all my fault. I shouldn't have tried. He said he had me. He said I could let go of the wall. I should've known better."

"Stop." Jane's voice slices through my spiral. "Absolutely not. We are not doing the Kayla Self-Blame Olympics tonight."

I press my hand to my forehead. "Jane—"

"No. Listen to me."

She takes a breath.

"Tell me the worst possible date someone could take you on."

I don't even have to think. "Something where the ground moves under me without my control. Or something with fast visual movement."

"Right," she says. "And what happened tonight?"

I close my eyes. "Both."

"Exactly."

Her voice softens.

"So the worst already happened. And you survived it."

I swallow hard.

"If this is a deal breaker for him," she continues, "you know now. You don't have to drag it out while you get more attached. And if it's not a deal breaker... then he's the right guy for you."

My throat tightens. "I just... I don't want to hope."

"Too late," she says gently. "You already do."

I wipe my eyes.

I hate that she's right.

But I know I needed her wisdom right now.

JACE

I'm still replaying the fall in my head when I get home.

Not just the fall —the moment *before* it.

The moment my body froze. The moment I couldn't move. The moment I failed her.

Anna's in the kitchen, making tea. She looks up. "Hey. How was the date?"

I drop into a chair. "A disaster."

She freezes. "What happened?"

"I took her ice skating," I say, rubbing my face. "She panicked. Completely. She fell. She cried. I didn't protect her. I didn't see it coming. I should've—"

"Whoa, slow down."

Anna sets her mug down and sits across from me. "Tell me exactly what you did."

I explain the rink, the teaching, the moment I pulled her from the wall, the fall, the meltdown.

I don't tell her about the freeze. Not yet. I can barely admit it to myself.

Anna's eyes widen.

She drops her cup.

"Oh crap—sorry—" She grabs a towel, then looks at me with a wince. "Jace... Kayla has sensory processing difficulties. Especially with movement and visual overload."

I stare at her. "So I took her on the worst date possible for her."

Anna winces again. "Yeah. Pretty much."

I groan and drop my head into my hands. "I messed everything up."

"No," she says firmly. "You didn't know. And you didn't leave her. You stayed. That matters."

I shake my head. "I didn't stay right away."

She frowns. "What do you mean?"

I swallow hard. “When she fell... I froze. I couldn’t move. I couldn’t think. I just—”I break off, shame burning through me. “I should’ve caught her. I should’ve helped faster. I should’ve— protected her.”

“Jace.” Anna’s voice is gentle but firm. “Freezing is a trauma response. Not a character flaw. And from what I know of Kayla she would understand that.”

I look up, startled.

She continues, “You’ve been through hell. You watched someone get hurt on the ice. Of course your body reacted. That doesn’t mean you failed her.”

I want to believe her. I can’t.

“Do you think she’ll ever want to see me again?” I ask quietly.

Anna smiles softly. “Absolutely, yes. She wouldn't have said yes in the first place if she didn't want to go out with you. If you care about her... ask her.”

I nod slowly.

I do care.

More than I should.

And the truth hits me like a punch:

I’m not just afraid she’ll reject me.

I’m afraid I’ll hurt her again.

Chapter Thirty-Three

The Explosion

Real listening isn't about hearing the words someone says — it's about noticing the weight behind them. Most people don't speak their truth out loud. They speak it in tremors, pauses, and the things they're trying not to fall apart over..

Mickey's Blog Bits

Jace

The room feels warm today — not temperature-wise, just... familiar. Parents chatting. Kids drifting between sensory stations. The usual hum of tired people doing their best.

Kayla waves from across the room, nervous, hopeful, timid and something in my chest loosens.

Then the door suddenly crashes open.

A woman steps in, clutching a folder like it's the only thing keeping her upright. She looks pale, hollow — like sleep hasn't touched her in days.

"Is this A Cuppa Support?" she says in a rush.

We don't have walk-ins but this woman clearly needs support.

Angela moves toward her instantly. "Hi, I'm Angela. Welcome. What's your name?"

"H-Helen," she whispers.

“Welcome, Helen. Usually, you get assigned to a group starting soon but why don't you sit and join us. Let me introduce you to everyone.”

We settle into the circle and Angela quickly introduces everyone. Helen sits stiffly, hands trembling in her lap, nodding to people as they are announced.

Angela starts softly. “We usually begin with a check-in. How’s everyone doing this week?”

There are tired laughs, a few groans.

Priya tells a story about Joshua disappearing until she found him on the roof. Anna says she is doing better now after Harry's diagnosis and Liam has handled it even better than her. Janette shares that Louise got an award at school.

Then Helen speaks.

“My daughter was diagnosed with autism last year,” she says, voice cracking. “She... she stopped going to school. She’s been so depressed. And now she is self-harming. I don’t know what to do. And my son is very angry. I think I’m struggling with depression myself. I don’t know how to help them. I don’t know if I can.”

The room goes still.

Priya leans forward. “My son refused school for months. He’s anxious all the time. You’re not alone.”

Tom nods. “My daughter used to have anxiety so bad she couldn’t leave the house. It felt like it would never get better. I felt like I was failing. Slowly, with a lot of help, we made it through.”

Helen’s eyes fill. “I feel like I’m failing her.”

Sarah’s boyfriend clears his throat — a quiet sound, but enough to draw attention. He hasn’t spoken much in the few sessions he has come, but tonight there’s something steady in the way he sits forward.

“I, uh... I don’t talk a lot in these meetings,” he begins, rubbing his palms together. “But I wanted to say something for Helen. Something I wish someone had said to me a year ago.”

Helen looks up, hopeful.

“My eldest,” he says softly, “is autistic. And he’s... well, he’s trans. He came out to me last year.”

A ripple moves through the group — not judgment, just surprise. This is new territory for them.

He continues, voice warm and honest.

"I know it's different, but how it affected me I think is similar. I didn't know anything about gender stuff. I didn't grow up around it. I still don't understand it. And I'm still scared I'll get it wrong. But he was struggling. Really struggling. And there was the occasional self-harm. But the moment I stopped trying to 'figure it out' and just started loving him exactly as he was... things got better. He was willing to go to therapy after that and he said it was because I didn't judge him, instead I found someone who could help him and me understand."

He glances at Helen, gentle and steady.

"You don't have to know everything to help your kid. You just have to stay connected. Keep showing up. Keep listening. That's what makes the difference. And find help that your daughter will feel comfortable accepting."

Sarah squeezes his knee, pride softening her features.

The room exhales — a collective release of tension none of them realised they were holding. We all like Dave and had no idea that he had experienced that.

Helen wipes her cheeks. "Thank you," she whispers. "I... I needed to hear that. I need to get therapy as well. I'm letting her down."

"I understand," I say quietly. "I've been struggling with anxiety and depression. I started therapy recently and it's helping. Feeling lost and overwhelmed doesn't mean you're failing. It means you care."

Anna adds softly, "I've been struggling since Harry's diagnosis. It's terrifying. But you're here. That matters."

Helen looks at us like she wants to believe it.

And then Martha jumps in.

"You need to read *Our Autistic Journey*," she says brightly, already pulling out her phone. "Mickey's post about her suicide attempt? That one? Let me find it — it's so helpful."

Kayla winces and goes to open her mouth, hesitation flashing across her face.

Before I can work out what she's thinking, Martha sees it and reacts instantly.

“Oh don’t start. I know you don’t like the blog. You always have something to say about it.”

The room freezes.

Kayla’s face goes white.

“Martha,” Angela warns softly.

But Martha barrels on, voice cracking. “My daughter read it during her worst moment. She was self-harming and suicidal. She said it was the first time she felt understood. She was on a 24-hour watch for days before it.”

Tears spill down Martha’s face. She’s spiralling.

“You don’t get to criticise something that saved my child. You don’t get to—”

“Martha,” I say, firmer. “Stop.”

She blinks, startled by her own volume.

And then her voice breaks completely.

“My daughter was suicidal,” she whispers. “She was cutting. She hated herself. And that blog — that post — kept her alive. I just... I just wanted to help Helen.”

Silence.

Angela moves instantly. “Okay. Thank you for sharing that. Let’s take a moment.”

She signals to the play leader. “Cyou take the children outside for a bit?”

The kids are ushered out. Parents follow to check on them. The room empties slowly.

Except for Kayla.

I try to get her to come with me, but she tells me to go check on Harry and Anna.

When I reach outside, I glance back through the windows — and I’m not the only one watching.

Kayla finally stands.

And to everyone's shock — including mine — she walks straight to Martha.

Martha flinches, expecting anger.

Instead, Kayla wraps her arms around her. A soft, steady hug.

Martha breaks. Sobs into Kayla's shoulder. Kayla holds her like she's holding something fragile and precious.

After a minute, Martha pulls away, wiping her face. I can't hear what they're saying, but Martha's shoulders loosen, and Kayla gives her a gentle smile.

Martha leaves the room, still shaken.

A few minutes later, she returns to the group outside and apologises — to everyone.

Kayla steps out after her, composed but pale.

"It's alright," she tells the group softly. "Really. It was just a misunderstanding, the subject was very sensitive for her. And I'm fine. I agree with Martha that post may be helpful."

Everyone exhales.

The crisis settles.

Angela, who has spent time integrating Helen into the group, making sure she's okay, introduces her to Martha and then walks over to Kayla. They talk quietly — deeply — and Angela's expression shifts from concern to surprise to excitement.

I'm not usually this nosy, but I just want to protect her.

Angela turns to the group. "If we'd like to continue, I received permission from Mickey to use the blog Martha mentioned in the group. It's a longer one and subject is triggering, so feel free to stay with the children if you'd prefer."

Kayla turns to the group. "Angela's asked me to read it, but I have an appointment at two, so I'll need to leave straight after."

She packs her bag with careful, deliberate movements.

She looks steady, but I can see the tremor in her hands.

All the parents choose to return to the meeting. I wait for Kayla to move, but instead she steps toward me.

She reaches into her bag and pulls out a ticket. A Perth Thunder ticket.

She holds it out to me. “I thought... maybe you’d like to go. You can fill in what I don’t know about the game.”

My chest warms. “Sounds great. I’d love that.”

“Just don’t try to get me on the ice,” she laughs — small, real, the first lightness I’ve seen from her all day.

I grimace. “No danger of that. I’ve learned my lesson. I’ll check the date plans with you first next time.”

She pauses. Looks at me like she wants to say something else but isn’t ready yet.

“We better go in, JP,” she says softly.

And I follow behind her, holding the ticket, feeling... hopeful.

The Darkest Hours

Trigger Warning

The following chapter contains **references to suicidal ideation, depression, and childhood emotional abuse**.

It does not describe any method of physical self-harm.

You may skip this chapter and continue to the next without losing narrative continuity.

The author believes that people experiencing suicidal thoughts should be supported by qualified mental health professionals.

Family and friends can be a consistent presence, but they also need boundaries and support of their own.

Chapter Thirty-Four

Surviving the Darkest Hours

Kayla

I sit down, open the blog, and begin reading.

Mickey

Today I found this in an old notebook and thought I would share it. I wrote it when I was fourteen and a half years old.

> Dear Diary, that's how this is meant to go, right? Not like I get anything else right. I tried to kill myself last week. I cried for hours. Then bitterness surged through me. Then nothing. Just numb. The words and memories in my head never stopped. Some of them were on a loop.

Others came all at once, like being hit from every direction. Mum and Dad arguing. Mum screaming, *"Pack your bags, we're leaving!"* Dad storming in, face furious, spitting venom:

"Are you happy now? It's all your fault."

I wish I could say I heard that once — a single moment that scarred me. But it was a recurring event. A soundtrack. Last week I closed the toilet door — the only safe place in the house — and slid down the wall. And the voices drowned me.

"You can't do anything right."
"Go cry in your room. I hate sooks."
"Your sister got 99% and she plays all day."
"Are you happy now? It's all your fault."
"Don't do that, everyone can see you."
"You're not good at anything."
"You were nine stone last year and now you're ten. You'll be sixteen stone at sixteen."
"Bad at sport. Bad at school. Fat and ugly."
"You're useless."
"Stop sooking."
"They don't love you as much as your sisters."
"Why can't you girls just do as I ask?"
"They'd be better off without you."
Mum screams, *"Pack your bags, we're leaving."*
Dad growls, *"Are you happy now? It's all your fault?"*
"You're a failure."
"You just make everyone miserable."
"Are you happy now? It's all your fault?"
"They would be happier without you."
"You don't add anything but pain."
"You make everyone miserable."
"You cause so much trouble." "It's all your fault."
"It's all your fault." "It's all your fault."
I'm sorry, God.
I know it's wrong. But I can't do this anymore.

The voices are quieter now, but they're still there. And there's a new one: *You're so useless, you couldn't even kill yourself."*

I think I might be crazy. But you don't talk about crazy in this house. You push it down. No emotions allowed. I'm already the sook. "Lucky you're a girl," Mum says. "Your dad would never let a boy be a sook."

Mum's calling. I don't know if I have the strength to listen to all her problems today, or which of my sisters' friends are being abused at home. But it's been like this since I was 10. Hopefully it's just about how annoying my sister or Dad is being. I have to go.

— Mickey, age 14

Kayla

As I finish the diary entry, I take in the room without lifting my eyes. There are tears everywhere. You can hear people holding their breath.

I push on. It can't end here.

Mickey aged 28

I reread this today before sharing it. I don't cry anymore when I read it. I'm not angry anymore.

I wish I could go back to fourteen-year-old me and tell her it's going to be alright. But I know she wouldn't have been able to hear it.

Have you ever heard the song *Standing With You* by Guy Sebastian? If not, I encourage you to listen to it.

That song is all about just being there beside someone struggling, no pressure, no confrontation, just a constant friendly presence. There's a line in it about the world not being better without you — oh how that line reminds me of that time.

When I listen to that song, I know that's what fourteen-year-old me needed. Not advice. Not solutions. Just someone willing to sit beside her in the dark and say:

"I'm not leaving."

I couldn't express how I felt back then. No one could have understood my mind at that point. But I needed to know I wasn't alone.

I can't tell you what it's like for everyone in that moment, but the songwriter's understanding in that song is profound to me. It captures something I didn't have words for.

How I wish I could tell fourteen-year-old Mickey that the world is not a better place without her. That one day she will look back and see every life she touched. Every person who thanked her for her kindness. Every child she helped. Every parent she supported. Every friend she held together.

The world needs you, Mickey. It needs your sensitive heart, your unique perspective, your beautiful soul.

You will surprise yourself with how intelligent you are. With how many people will look to you for advice. With the lives you will see transform because of your compassion and your work.

So to my readers

If you know someone struggling with depression or suicidal thoughts, please encourage them to seek support from a counsellor or psychologist if they're willing.

But just as important is this:

Be there. Sit with them. Help with daily tasks. Do activities together. Let them know they are not alone.

Sometimes the smallest presence can be the thing that keeps someone here.

Kayla

I lift my head finally.

There are wet eyes everywhere. People have moved to comfort each other. Angela is already in motion, grounding the room, making sure everyone is okay.

Across the room, I hear Martha whisper, "Thank you."

I smile at her — small, soft — and quietly leave the room.

Chapter Thirty-Five

Struggling to Justify

> "I used to feel guilty for taking even a small moment for myself. We all walk around with invisible stories stitched under our skin. No one sees the weight we carry — and we don't see theirs. So taking a quiet moment to breathe, repair, or just exist isn't selfish. It's survival."
>
> Mickey's Blog Bits

Kayla

I didn't tell anyone my appointment was a nail appointment. Even now, I still struggle to justify self-care.

Once a month, I sit across from Nary while she works on my flimsy, paper-thin nails that split below the fingertip. It's not indulgence; it's repair. And it's the only time I get to sit still without someone needing something from me.

Nary knows me well enough not to fill the silence. She chats occasionally, but mostly she lets me drift. And today, my mind drifts straight back to the parent group — to the stories that spilled out of those parents, to the blog, to the weight of everything they carry.

I think about each of them. Their children. Their exhaustion. Their fear. Their resilience.

And I think about anyone daring to tell *them* — or their kids — to "toughen up," or "stop being so sensitive," or "just push through."

The rage rises so fast it almost startles me,

These people are my connection. My community. My people. I care about them — specifically them — and their children. I don't want anyone diminishing their struggles the way mine were diminished.

My counsellor would be thrilled that I'm actually feeling something instead of immediately turning it into data. Because that's what I do — I don't dissect emotions like a scientist; I process them like a data-entry clerk. Input. Categorise. File. Store. Impersonal. Efficient. Detached.

But today, I'm not filing anything. I'm sitting in it. And it's awful.

My childhood rises up like a memory I didn't ask for. I was always told to be tougher, stronger, less emotional. "You're too sensitive." "You're too dramatic." "Stop crying." Those words shaped me more than anyone realised.

And yes — my parents *were* the reason the house felt like a battlefield. Not because they were bad people, but because life hit us hard and none of us had the tools. My sister's cancer at thirteen. My puberty at eight. The exhaustion that swallowed my parents whole. The way attention narrowed to survival.

I adore my dad. People don't understand that because I often talk about how his realism felt like criticism. But he was consistent. Predictable. He let me argue back. Sometimes he even conceded — which was monumental for him. He showed love through doing, through providing, through protecting.

He's autistic ADHD — undiagnosed, but obvious. Not unapologetic, but *in your space, in your face* — impossible to ignore. His flaws aren't hidden; they're right there, loud and present.

My mum... everyone said she was a great mother. Even my sister's friends called her Mum. I loved her. But I spent my whole life trying not to be her, trying not to be emotional like her. I didn't want to feel everything so intensely. I didn't want to be the mother she was. So I learned to intellectualise. I can't bottle emotions like my sister can — mine spill out whether I want them to or not. But once they're out, I sort them, label them, file them away before they can cause damage.

Today, I'm letting them sit. I hate it.

When Martha screamed at me, I froze. I was only going to share my own experience — intrusive thoughts, depression, the things I've lived with quietly. But the more she yelled, the more I recognised her pain. It wasn't about me. It was everything inside her bursting at once.

I don't know what her issue is with me, and honestly, I don't care. That's her problem. It's taken years to be able to say that and mean it. But I also know she's human, and she was hurting.

As the others moved outside, I walked toward her and crouched beside her. She flinched. I rested my hand lightly on her arm. Her whole body was curled in on itself, shaking.

I stayed until my legs cramped, then shifted to a chair.

"Martha," I said softly, "I don't want to make this about me. I can see you're in a lot of pain. But I think you misunderstood me. I have my own journey with mental health. I've worked with teens who struggle. I can't imagine what it's like to be a parent in your situation."

She cried harder, but her body loosened.

"I imagine — from my daughter's OCD — that you feel helpless. Frustrated. Like there's nothing you can do."

She nodded, whispering yes through broken sobs.

"I'm glad the blog helped you and your daughter," I said. "I just... I know Mickey. She'd hate being put on a pedestal. She believes her voice is just one of many. But the important thing here is your daughter. If I can help either of you, tell me."

Her face — emotionally exhausted, grateful — is something I won't forget.

I told her I'd let the group know everything was fine, just big emotions. She addressed them briefly, then left. I read the blog afterward, and now here I am, sitting in this discomfort, letting it rise and pass.

You never know what people are carrying. You never know their backstory. You never know what makes them the way they are in any given moment.

And that's what terrifies me about Jace.

Most people give up before they understand me, before I can open up. Here's a secret I don't tell anyone: I could love anyone as long as they loved me. I'm a lifer. Once you know me, accept me, you have me for life. You'd have to do something truly terrible to break that.

But other people aren't like that. They're indecisive. Impulsive. Their feelings shift. Their intentions change. Mine don't. Once I decide, I decide. My babies' names never changed. My future plans stayed set. Once you're my friend... and my partner even more so.

It had been a brutal week. I'm an intervention teacher; I work with children carrying trauma, and sometimes I wish I could just sit down and teach literacy and numeracy like everyone else. But I can't ignore what I see. I can't pretend trauma isn't strangling their learning. And when no one else steps in to help them, something inside me breaks.

I wish I were the kind of person who could shelve it, detach, and just do the job. But I'm not. I advocate. I speak up. I put myself on the line for these kids. And then I get brushed off — *what would I know, I'm just a tutor.* A tutor. As if my Masters of Education and years of training in trauma, behaviour, and counselling don't exist. As if I'm overreacting instead of seeing what's right in front of us.

So yes, it's been a hard week. Martha's comments were barely a blip in the pile of everything else.

And somewhere in all of that, I'm reminded that I don't want to keep putting my heart out there. I don't want to keep being crushed by other people's indecision, impulsivity, or ignorance. I don't want to keep being overlooked because someone can't see my worth. That's why relationships terrify me. That's why I don't want to give in to these thoughts about Jace.

The problem is Jace has never seemed impulsive or indecisive. He's standing at a crossroads in his life, letting the options settle before choosing a direction. It's wise — I know it is. But still, I'm afraid of being hurt again.

The beginning of relationships has always been the hardest part for me. People feel like puzzles; I need enough pieces before I can see the picture clearly, before I can interpret each moment and respond the right way. Maybe a second date would give me more data.

But he's too young or younger than me. He hasn't had children, and I can't have any more. On paper — in a neat little pros-and-cons column — he'd be the worst possible choice.

But when I get past the brutal logic installed in me since birth, I reach a truth that terrifies me. He makes me feel safe, seen, valuable. He is someone I would genuinely choose to spend time with, even if romance wasn't part of the equation. But that terrifies me because in my world those things have never lasted.

Frank has already completed the risk assessment. The intrusive voice has contributed seventeen worst-case scenarios. The rest of my internal committee seems determined to hold an emergency meeting. I need them all to take the afternoon off.

But I'm glad I gave him the tickets today because now it's out of my hands. Time to deal with my fears and give this a real chance to succeed.

Chapter Thirty-Six

Perth Thunder

There's a strange kind of magic in discovering that the thing you feared would break you becomes the moment that opens you instead.
Mickey's Blog Bits

Jace

I get to the arena early.

Not because I'm excited — though I am — but because I'm nervous. The good kind. The kind that makes you check your reflection in the glass doors even though you know you look exactly the same as you did in the car.

Kayla arrives right on time.

She spots me, lifts a hand in a small wave, and something in my chest eases. She looks calm, but her shoulders are tight, her steps measured. She's nervous too.

"Hey," I say.

"Hi." She tucks a strand of hair behind her ear. "Thanks for coming."

"Thanks for inviting me."

We both laugh — awkward, but not uncomfortable. Just... new.

Inside the foyer, the noise hits us — the echo of voices, the buzz of the crowd, the thump of music from the rink.

Kayla pauses.

Not freezing. Not panicking. Just taking stock.

"I should tell you something," she says quietly. "I have sensory processing differences. Noise, movement, unpredictability — they can cause really high levels of anxiety for me. The ice skating... it created a sensory overload."

I nod. "I didn't know. I wouldn't have" I falter. Wouldn't have taken her? Planned the date? Asked her out? None of it sounds right.

"You couldn't have known." She gives a small shrug. "I'm not avoiding things because I don't want to do them. Some things I just need to prepare for, and others... I need to choose the timing myself."

"Thank you for telling me," I say, and I mean it.

She exhales, relieved. "I'd be happy to watch you and Harry skate. Or if you wanted to take my kids skating, I'd watch happily. Though Archie has the same sensory responses I do."

That makes me smile. "Good to know. I'll keep him off the ice."

She huffs a laugh, and some of the tension leaves her shoulders.

"Does Mickey get stuff wrong about the sensory side of things? Is that why you don't like her blog?" I ask.

She stiffens, and my mouth gets ahead of my brain — trying to smooth it over.

"I read the blog Martha mentioned," I add quickly. "It's amazingly written. A lot of the posts helped me. But if you have a reason—"

Kayla cuts in gently. "No, I think it's fantastic that the blog helps people. But it's just one story about autistic life. People are complex. We're all different. I just want people to read other stories too, or we end up creating a new set of stereotypes about what autistic life looks like, feels like, and what supports are needed."

She pauses, then adds with a dry, exaggerated wary look, "Martha misunderstood my intention. I explained it to her. Honestly, I'm relieved to understand why it was so important to her. She seemed a bit... obsessive before that."

I laugh, and she smiles.

"I've had a chance to get to know Martha," she says. "She seemed so invulnerable that I didn't try to connect with her."

I murmur my agreement, wondering if I'd made the same mistake with Kayla — assuming she didn't need anyone.

I'm about to ask if she chose this date to make up for the ice rink disaster.

But then the game starts.

And everything I thought I knew shifts.

The puck drops.
The crowd roars.

And Kayla — quiet, careful, controlled Kayla — becomes one of the loudest voices in the entire arena.

She's on her feet.
She's clapping.

She's yelling, "THAT WAS OFFSIDE, OPEN YOUR EYES!" with the confidence of someone who's been watching hockey for years.

I stare at her.

She doesn't notice.
She's too busy cheering.

When she finally sits, she leans toward me. "Okay, explain that play. Why did they reset the face off?"

"Ref ruled the puck was frozen before the rebound," I say.

She nods like she's filing it away. "And why did they change lines so fast when they were doing so well?"

"Shift rotation. You don't want to gas your forwards."

She grins. "That makes sense."

And she means it.

She's not pretending.
She's not performing.
She's not doing this for me.

She's genuinely enjoying herself.

And I realise — sharply, unexpectedly — that she didn't choose this date to please me.

She chose it because she likes the sport.
She likes learning.
She likes being here. She likes being here with me.

By the second period, we're leaning closer without noticing.
By the third, we're sharing jokes about the goalie's terrible glove hand.
By overtime, it feels like we've known each other longer than a few weeks.

When the Thunder score the winning goal, Kayla jumps to her feet and cheers so loudly the guy in front of us flinches.

I laugh — I can't help it.

She looks at me, cheeks flushed, eyes bright. "Sorry. I get enthusiastic."

"Don't apologise," I say. "I like it."

Her smile softens.

Something in my chest shifts.

We walk out into the cool night air, still buzzing from the game.

I don't want the night to end.

"Kayla?" I say.

She looks up at me.

"Would you... want to be my girlfriend? Start dating regularly. Properly."

She stops walking.

Her face goes still — not cold, just processing.

"I'm not good at relationships," she says quietly. "But I like you."

My heart thuds.

She continues, voice steady but vulnerable in a way I know costs her something.

"I need you to be honest with me at all times. If you're having doubts, or you want to change this from being serious or long term, you need to tell me straight away. Even if you think it will hurt me. It probably will. But if you're honest, I can get through it."

I reach for her hand and wait for her to glance back up at me.

"I will be honest with you. Always," I say sincerely.

She's still looking at me affectionately after I tell her I'll always be honest. Really looking. The noise of the game fades a little, like the whole rink steps back to give us space. She's close — close enough that I can feel her breath when she exhales. Her eyes flick down to my mouth for half a second, and my chest tightens.

I lean in a little without meaning to. She doesn't move away. If anything, she shifts closer. I know exactly how big this moment is. I reach up and gently touch her chin so she can see my face clearly. Her lips part just a little, like she's ready for whatever comes next.

We're right there — one breath away — when her stomach growls. Loud.

She freezes. Then her face goes bright red and she lets out this tiny, mortified laugh. I can't help it — I burst out laughing too. The tension snaps in the best possible way.

"How about we get some food before heading back?" I say, still grinning.

She nods, smiling — really smiling. The kind of smile that hits me straight in the chest.

"Yeah. I'd like that."

And for the first time in a long time, it feels like something in my life is finally moving in the right direction.

Chapter Thirty-Seven

Hopes and Fears

The marks that don't bruise. Some harm never shows on skin. It shows in hesitation, in silence, in the quiet planning you do when no one is watching. Those marks last the longest.

Mickey's Blog Bits

Kayla

The two weeks after the Thunder game felt steady in a way I wasn't used to. Jace and I were finding a rhythm — slow, calm, uncomplicated. I liked it. I liked him. But the more comfortable I felt, the more the old fears crept in around the edges. Not loudly. Just enough to make me second-guess myself, second-guess him, second-guess the idea that something good could actually stay good.

I needed grounding. Helping a friend set up a new house and settle in felt like a good way to do that. By the time I arrived at Priya's place, the hopes and fears were swirling quietly in the background, and I was ready to focus on whatever she needed. Priya's new rental smells faintly musty — the kind of old-tenant scent that clings to carpet and cupboards that haven't been opened in months. But the kids don't seem to mind. They're outside exploring the tiny backyard like it's a whole adventure, voices bright and safe in a way that makes my chest loosen.

Inside, we're surrounded by flat-pack furniture, half-assembled bed frames, and instructions that look like they were drawn by someone who has never met a screwdriver. My hands ache from forcing bolts into misaligned holes, and Priya's hair is falling out of her bun in exhausted waves.

We finally collapse onto the floor, backs against the wall, drinking instant coffee because the kettle is the only appliance she owns so far.

Priya exhales shakily. "I can't believe this is happening."

I nudge her shoulder. "You did it."

She stares at the half-built bed frame. "I didn't take anything from the old house. Not even the kids' beds."

"That's wise," I say softly. I'd heard her and Sarah talking for weeks about trying to get second-hand furniture off Marketplace and storing it at Sarah's place. Priya had been secretly selling small items from her own house — only the ones her husband wouldn't notice — just to scrape together enough money to replace the things the kids needed. What she didn't know was that most of us were already aware of what was happening. We'd quietly pooled money, set up a fund, and asked Sarah to 'find a great deal' so Priya wouldn't feel exposed. It wasn't much, but it was more than she could have managed with the tiny amount of money her husband didn't control. We understood her decision and need to leave.

She swallows. "He would've stopped me. Controlled the whole thing. And the kids still need beds when they're with him. I'm not trying to take them away. I just... want them to have a better life."

I nod. "You're giving them safety. That matters more than furniture."

Priya's eyes glisten. "It's strange. The marks that don't leave bruises are the ones that stay the longest."

We sit quietly for a moment, letting the truth settle.

Then she turns her head and studies me with that unnervingly perceptive gaze she has. "You look lighter."

I blink. "Lighter how?"

"Kayla," she says, a teasing softness in her voice, "you're dating Jace. Officially. That tends to make people lighter."

Heat creeps up my neck. "I haven't had a good history with relationships."

Priya nods slowly. "I can see that. People don't understand you and they—"

"Don't take the time for me to let them in," I finish, my head bowing, my face tightening in that uncomfortable, contorted way I hate — the way that feels like being seen too clearly.

Priya's voice softens. "Exactly. But Jace seems to be giving you time."

I swallow. "He's easy to be around."

She raises an eyebrow. "Easy?"

I huff a laugh. "Fine. He's steady. He doesn't push." I pause, trying to find the words.

Priya cuts in gently, "Doesn't treat your differences like inconveniences."

"Differences?" I squeak — a small, nervous sound I hate, my voice tightening as my shoulders lift slightly. My face tenses, unsure what she's seen, unsure how much she knows, unsure if I should be embarrassed or relieved.

Priya gives me a look — soft, knowing, warm. The kind that says *I know. You don't have to hide.* That's it. Nothing more than that.

And strangely, it feels safe... even though I'm still nervous. My throat tightens.

"He remembers things," I say quietly. "Real things. Like how I take my coffee. Or that Archie hates crying — so he gently steers him away from loud kids instead of telling him to toughen up."

Priya's expression softens. "He sees you."

I nod. "Yeah. He does."

"And you see him."

I take a breath — the kind that feels like stepping onto thin ice.

"I see that he's struggling," I say quietly. "With life away from hockey. With adapting to Australia. With not being needed as much by Anna and Liam now that things are calmer. He's... used to being the person who steps in and fixes things."

Priya listens, still and attentive.

"And I'm scared," I admit. "That maybe he's drawn to me because I look like something that needs fixing. Me. My kids. My life. And once everything is stable, he'll realise he doesn't actually want me — he just wanted the chaos."

Priya's response is immediate, firm but gentle. "There is nothing to fix."

I look at her, unsure.

She continues, "And I do not think he sees you that way at all. Not even a little."

My chest tightens — not in panic, but in something fragile and hopeful.

"We have a lot in common," I say softly. "Which is weird. He's athletic and I'm... the opposite. But we share the same interests. Even with sport — I like watching, and he plays at a level a girlfriend could never meet anyway. I never thought I'd be with an athlete."

Priya laughs — a real, warm laugh that fills the room. "Kayla, you are full of surprises."

I roll my eyes, but I'm smiling too.

"I'm trying," I whisper.

Priya reaches over and squeezes my hand. "That's all you've ever needed to do."

We sit there until the coffee goes cold, until the kids burst back inside asking for snacks, until the afternoon light shifts into gold.

Before I leave, I turn to her. "Priya... I'm here. For anything. Anytime. You don't have to do any of this alone."

Her eyes soften. "Thank you. Really."

And for the first time in a long time, I feel like I am surrounded by people who see me, really see me and accept me as I am.

Chapter Thirty-Eight

Opportunities

Wrong place, right time. Life has a way of dropping you in the wrong place at the right moment. A rink. A conversation. A door left open you didn't expect. And suddenly you're rethinking everything.

Mickey's Blog Bits

Jace

Dating Kayla feels different. Simple. Steady. Real.

Two weeks in, and I keep catching myself thinking about her at random times — when I'm brushing my teeth, when I'm cooking, when I'm trying to fall asleep. Not big dramatic thoughts, just small flashes of her. The way she leans into me on the couch. The way she laughs when she's trying not to. The way she relaxes when I put a hand on her back.

She responds to my touch easily — not crossing any lines, just moving with me without thinking. And yeah, I feel it. I'm a guy; my body reacts before my brain does. There are moments where I know I could take things further and she'd follow without hesitation. But she needs this to be slow. She needs certainty. So, I slow myself down. I keep things steady. It's not always easy — not when every part of me wants to pull her closer — but if I want this to last, and I do, then slow is the only option.

My mind drifts to the way she kissed me last week — soft, sure, like she meant it. The way her lips moved against mine, the way her hand slid up my chest, the way she fit against me when I pulled her in. My hand had settled around her waist, and she'd leaned into it like she'd been waiting for it. I groaned under my breath just thinking about it. Not helpful, brain.

Another moment flashes through my head — that night on her couch when she shifted closer, her thigh brushing against mine, and looked up at me like she was waiting for something. I'd tucked a strand of hair behind her ear and she'd sucked in a breath, barely noticeable but enough to hit me straight in the chest. She leaned into my hand like she didn't even realise she was doing it. And yeah, my whole body reacted. Hard not to. I had to pull back a little, breathe, remind myself to slow down. I groaned just thinking about it.

I think about that moment in her kitchen — the one where I reached past her to grab a glass and she stepped back right into me. My hand landed on her hip before I even realised what I was doing, and my whole body reacted. She felt it. I know she did. Her face went bright red and she hid her face in her hands, mumbling, "Sorry," in this tiny squeak of a voice. "I'm not ready—" "I know," I cut in, because I did. She nodded, still flustered, still pink, and stepped away so fast she nearly bumped the counter. And yeah, I'd been flustered too. I'd had to plant my hands on the bench and breathe for a second. Mentally, I counted Ten Mississippis while mentally repainting a porch.

I think I've shown more self-control in the last two weeks than I managed in the previous thirty-three years.

The agony is killing me.

A car honks in the distance and I'm bought back to the present. Sitting in my car outside the ice rink. My brain and body really need to chill and focus on what i am doing.

I'm still figuring out what to do today, just like I'm trying to figure out the rest of my life.

I miss hockey. Not the travel or the pressure — just the ice. The locker room. The feeling of being part of something. I miss being useful. Being someone people rely on.

Which is probably why I ended up at the rink today. Habit. Comfort. Something familiar. I force myself to move from the car to the inside of the rink and then to the cafe inside.

I was grabbing a coffee when one of the rink staff I talk to regularly spotted me and waved me over. I figured he just wanted to chat, but then he looked across the rink and went, "Oh — perfect timing." He nodded toward a guy in a Thunder jacket. "I've been meaning to introduce you two. He's here with his daughter — figure skating practice." Before I could ask anything, the guy walked over. He appeared to recognise me. It's possible it was from my time in the NHL, after all I wasn't a nobody in hockey.

But he could only know I was in Perth because the rink staff had mentioned it. Total coincidence. Wrong place, right time.

We shook hands, and I looked at him, curious why they seemed so eager for me to meet him. Then he said, "Heard Seattle reached out." I froze. He saw it. "The rink manager's a friend," he added. "He thinks you'd be a great fit at the Thunder." He sounded almost like he was trying to recruit me. But he was just here because his kid skates... right? Except he wasn't looking at me like a parent. He was looking at me like an asset — someone worth keeping — and he was curious enough to see if there was anything that might make me stay. He knew he couldn't offer anything close to Seattle. He didn't pretend otherwise. But he was feeling out whether there was something else I wanted. Something that wasn't about money or league status. I'd been in enough negotiations to recognise the dance, but I still couldn't imagine what they could possibly want me for here in Perth. The ice hockey scene here wasn't anywhere near the scale of the NHL, and most of the staff were volunteers. Truthfully, I'd be happy to volunteer — but I needed a real job.

He didn't push. Didn't pitch anything. Just left the door open.

I stood there for a minute after he walked off, thinking about everything — Seattle, Perth, hockey, family, identity.

And Kayla.

She's part of this now. I have never been the kind of guy to randomly date, when I decide to start a relationship, I intend for it to go the distance. I'll admit I wasn't thinking about America when I suggested we start a relationship. I was in denial, which isn't normally me. I just knew I wanted to be with her and I didn't want to think about the complications.

She's steady. She's thoughtful. She's careful with me in a way I didn't know I needed.

And when she leans into me — even just her shoulder brushing mine — something in me settles. Something that's been restless for years.

I don't know what the future looks like. I don't know what I'm supposed to choose. I don't know how to map out the path forward.

But I know one thing clearly:

I don't want to lose what's happening with her.

Not now. Not when it finally feels like I'm finally finding a life beyond hockey.

Chapter Thirty-Nine

Life Wasn't Meant to Be Like the Movies

> *People think heartbreak comes from betrayal. But sometimes it comes from a single moment where your brain whispers, "See? You were never safe," and every wall you worked so hard to lower slams back into place.*
>
> Mickey's Blog Bits

Kayla

one week later

Three weeks of dating Jace. Three weeks of slow steps, careful pacing, and not giving more than I got. Three weeks of him meeting me exactly where I was — not pushing, not pulling, just... steady. I can't remember a time when I have laughed so much and felt seen, even though I'm hiding so much. I always have. But at least I'm not infatuated.

For the first time in my life, I wasn't sprinting into a relationship. I wasn't over-giving. I wasn't losing myself.

I was proud of that. And proud of us.

Tonight, the house is full — Liam, Anna, Harry, Violet, Aleia, Archie — all piled into my lounge room for movie night. I watched him talking with his brother, laughing at something I couldn't hear, and a quiet warmth settled through me — the kind that comes from remembering moments I hadn't let myself overthink.

I remembered the first time he kissed me. He'd paused first, giving me space to step back if I needed it. One hand rested at my waist, steady but not possessive, and the other cupped my cheek with a gentleness that made my breath catch. When he leaned in, it wasn't rushed or impulsive. It was careful — the kind of careful that comes from someone who actually sees me. Our lips met in a soft, searching kiss, a question and an answer all at once. I hadn't obsessed over it. I'd just let myself feel it.

I remembered the parent group meeting, all of us sitting around the tables discussing strategies and sharing stories. Our fingers brushed when we both reached for the same handout, then again when he passed me a pen. It wasn't deliberate, but the warmth of his touch lingered longer than it should have. I didn't analyse it or try to decode it. I just let the moment be what it was — simple, sweet, unexpectedly grounding.

I remembered the sunset on the hill, the sky melting into gold while he slid his arm around my shoulders. I'd leaned into him without worrying about what it meant or where it might lead. His warmth seeped into me, steady and calm, anchoring me in a way I wasn't used to. I didn't imagine futures or catastrophes. I just let myself enjoy the quiet.

I remembered sitting beside him on the couch, our knees touching as some movie played in the background. He'd tucked a strand of hair behind my ear, his fingers lingering for a heartbeat. Normally I would've dissected a gesture like that until the magic dissolved, but I didn't. I just let myself enjoy the closeness, the softness of it.

And I remembered the early-evening stroll with the kids, the sky dimming and the air cooling as we walked them around the block before bedtime. He'd slipped his hand into mine again, giving it a gentle squeeze like he was checking I was still there. I didn't chase meaning or try to predict the next chapter. I just held his hand back and let the moment be enough.

Standing there now, watching him with his brother, all those memories washed through me — soft, uncomplicated, and strangely comforting. I wasn't spiralling into fear or imagining a future. I was simply acknowledging that I'd liked those moments. That they'd mattered. That they'd felt good.

And for once, that was enough.

We moved to the lounge chairs, after the popcorn and snacks were served and put on the movie, *The Mighty Ducks*. The kids are half watching, half playing. The adults are half watching, half talking. It's warm. Familiar. Safe.

I'm curled into Jace on the lounge, his arm around me, my head on his chest. His heartbeat is steady. Comforting.

As the movie is coming to an end, Harry is asleep on a beanbag. Archie is blinking slow, heavy blinks. Violet and Aleia disappeared into my room half an hour ago with craft supplies.

This feels like a life I could belong to. For the first time in years, I wasn't waiting for the other shoe to drop. I let myself believe this could last.

Before Archie finally gives in to sleepiness, I help him up and walk him to his room. He leans against my shoulder — warm, trusting, and completely unaware of his weight. I stumble with him down the hallway until I finally get him onto the bed and tuck him in. I stroke his cheek and switch off the lamp.

When I walk back toward the lounge, I hear the conversations continuing.

I step into the kitchen — close enough to hear them, far enough that they can't see me — and grab a drink.

I'm about to return, tuning into their voices so I can join in, when I freeze. I can't hear everything — just enough to fill in the blanks with the worst possible versions.

Anna: "You have to tell her, Jace. She won't be okay with you not telling her about this. I would be livid if Liam didn't tell me. I mean — this coaching job in Seattle is one million a year, and what are all those phone calls with Mel."

My stomach drops.

What job? Seattle? Mel? America?

He's leaving? Mel?

He promised. He promised he'd be honest if things changed. He promised.

Jace in a quiet, tense voice bites out, "Anna, I have things sorted. The calls with Mel are none of your business. Let me handle—"

I can't hear the last words.

Handle what?

My chest tightens. My hands go cold.

"She's, my friend. I won't let you hurt her. Mel told me you just decided one day that was it and it was over. And why are you talking to her now — are you leading her on?" Anna mumbles in a sharp but hushed voice.

I step closer, just enough to see Jace's face.

Furious. Maybe guilty. Something I can't read.

Liam growls, "That's enough."

Silence.

I wait a minute — long enough that it won't look like I was listening — and then step forward.

Everyone snaps into fake casualness so fast it's almost insulting.

Anna smiles too brightly. Liam adjusts a cushion that didn't need adjusting. Jace stands like he's been caught doing something wrong. My brain labels it guilt, but I know that's not always accurate. Trauma makes everything look like a threat.

I swallow the lump in my throat.

"Hey guys..." My voice sounds normal. Too normal. "I'm tired and I'm feeling a bit off. Is it okay if we wrap it up early?" My body is already going into shutdown — heavy, slow, distant.

Anna nods immediately. "Of course. We'll check in tomorrow."

Jace steps toward me, leaning in for a kiss.

I step back.

"I don't want to get you sick," I say quickly, avoiding his eyes.

I can't talk to him like this. I'd either shut down completely or say something I can't take back.

He freezes.

I grab a blanket, a stray cup — anything to keep my hands busy, anything to keep my face turned away.

Everyone packs up quietly. No one says what they're thinking. No one asks what I heard. And I don't offer it.

Because if I open my mouth right now, I'm not sure what will come out.

When the door closes behind them, the house feels too quiet. Too empty. Too familiar.

The old ache settles in my chest.

Of course. Of course, this is what happens when I let myself hope.

Everything was going well. Too well.

I can feel the shutdown creeping in — cold, heavy, inevitable.

The moment everything breaks.

And the tears finally come.

Chapter Forty

The Cost of Help

> Some days it feels like the system wants proof that you're drowning before it throws you a life jacket. And then it asks you to fill out a form explaining why you needed one.
>
> Mickey's Blog Bits

Kayla

It's been a week since the movie night, and I keep telling myself I don't know what's going on. I keep hoping Jace will just tell me.

He's been busy, and my life is always chaos anyway — work, therapy appointments, independence-building tasks at home, school issues, coordinating disability support workers, checking that the people meant to help are actually helping — and none of that is for me.

All of it is necessary. All of it is work I would do a thousand times over for my kids.

But sometimes the making-it-happen is more work than the support itself. People don't see the endless efforts to avoid stressors and triggers. The careful balance of comforting and then stretching.

I've always said parenting is hard for everyone. But parenting disabled children can be isolating in a way most people never see. You lose friendships. You lose time. You lose the ability to hand your child to a family member or a friend for a break because their needs are too high or too misunderstood. You lose the way you would have gone about your day if you weren't avoiding meltdowns and ensuring the right balance of stimulation and rest.

Across the room, I see the same thing on every face. Not tired — worn.

Someone jokes that their holiday wasn't a break. Someone else laughs too loudly. Others don't laugh at all. It's too close to the truth.

Then the talk shifts — not to the kids, not to school, not to therapy — but to the thing everyone has been pretending not to think about since it hit the news.

The changes. The reviews. The new NDIS rules. And the whispers about "parental responsibility."

Priya leans forward, elbows on her knees. Anna rubs her temples. Someone wipes their eyes before the tears even fall.

Uncharacteristically, Tom speaks first.

"I can't believe the proposed subsections in the new NDIS bill — 34(1G) and (1H) about parental responsibility, and (IK) about ignoring family impact when assessing funding."

"(IJ)," Sarah corrects automatically.

"It's not like they considered family impact much before," I mutter. "And if they did, it wasn't consistent."

"What's the NDIS?" Jace asks, brow furrowed.

"National Disability Insurance Scheme — or NDIA, the agency," Sarah explains. "It's how people with disabilities get funding for living supports."

I see the concern on Jace's face, but I'm too fed up to try to explain it right now. I'm so tired of this. No one here hates the NDIS. No one wants to lose it. We all know funding increased with it — even if supports didn't always follow. We're just exhausted from fighting so hard for our kids to have a good life.

"What kind of supports?" Jace asks.

"Occupational therapy, physiotherapy, speech therapy, psychology, nurses, support workers, independent living, assistive technology — things relevant to the specific disability, based on the reports you provide," Priya says.

"Support worker?" Jace looks puzzled.

"A person who helps someone with daily functioning — in-home supports, community access, and activities that support therapy," Angela adds. "We had to fight really hard last plan to get Ari her support worker hours. With her cerebral palsy, it was suggested we get more nursing hours, but it's a different job."

"I spent months preparing for a planning meeting," I say, "just to have half the reports ignored. Meanwhile you'd see other families get high supports they didn't seem to need or use."

"We're grateful," Janette says softly. "We are. We know how lucky we are to have support at all."

Heads nod. No one here asks for more than they need.

"But the cost of getting it..." She shakes her head. "It's too high."

And then the stories begin.

Martha spent forty-three hours gathering reports for a review that were ignored. Tom knew a father whose son's violent meltdowns were dismissed as "ordinary parenting." Angela had to explain, again, why her daughter needs another adult to shower safely. Dave lost his job because he couldn't meet work-hour rules and still care for his grandson.

"They act like we're stealing from taxpayers," Anna says. "Like we're fraudsters."

"We're not stealing anything," Janette adds. "We're just trying to keep our kids safe."

I feel something in me snap.

"They say parents are the problem. But the real problems are the bureaucracy — the endless paperwork, the compliance rules, the reporting requirements. The companies say they have to charge more because of all the admin NDIS demands."

A few parents murmur in agreement.

"When NDIS first started," I say, "therapy prices were so high they were sometimes more than double what they'd been before. And it wasn't because therapists suddenly became twice as skilled. It was because the admin overheads exploded. The paperwork. The compliance. The reporting. The audits. The constant rule changes."

Heads nod. Everyone remembers.

"People without NDIS slowly couldn't access basic therapy anymore," I continue. "Prices went up across the whole sector because providers said they had to charge more to cover the admin burden. And somehow the blame still landed on parents — as if we were the ones driving up the costs, not the bureaucracy that made everything harder and more expensive."

I take a breath, but the frustration keeps rising.

"First, it was travel time plus travel cost. When that was removed, they said, 'We'll charge you an hour for forty-five minutes face-to-face and fifteen minutes of notes.' Then suddenly they needed another fifteen minutes of notes because the reporting requirements changed. So a forty-five-minute appointment became an hour and fifteen."

Someone groans. Someone else swears under their breath.

"And support work?" I add. "NDIS gives you an hour a day, but agencies won't do shifts under three hours because of their admin overheads. And somehow, we're meant to negotiate with companies who know we have no power. They say, 'Sorry, that's our minimum — blame NDIS.' And NDIS says, 'Sorry, negotiate with the provider.' And we're stuck in the middle."

I shake my head.

"I don't want to sound ungrateful. But parenting is already hard. Fighting endless systems and bureaucracy shouldn't be part of the job."

Jace squeezes my hand. I lean into him, needing the strength.

"I saw those newspaper articles blaming parents for NDIS fraud," he says quietly. "Somehow it always comes back to parents."

Martha nods. "We were told it gets easier when they start school. No one warned us we could be raising teenagers with the needs of three-year-olds. I don't know how you do it, Kayla. And Priya — no one cares that we never get a break."

She's come a long way. She's trying to connect now. It matters.

Silence settles. Not heavy — familiar.

Because every parent here knows the truth:

They love their kids. They would do anything for them. They already are doing everything for them.

But the system asks more. And more. And more.

Priya's voice cracks. "And when we finally say we need help, the answer is, 'You're asking for too much. You're a parent — that's your job.' As if we aren't already doing the work of three adults. As if we aren't already stretched past breaking."

"There was that case in the parliamentary inquiry," Sarah adds, "where a parent was told that if they couldn't care for their child's extra needs, the family would be reported to Child Protection — and that was by an NDIS representative in a planning meeting."

She pauses, then clarifies — the part that made every parent in the room go still.

"And not only that — it was said in response to their funding being cut. They questioned the cuts, explained they couldn't meet their child's needs without the supports, and the planner said, 'Well, if you can't care for them, we'll have to notify Child Protection.'"

A ripple of horror moves through the room. We all know this case would be an extreme — but the system hasn't been fair to us either.

My stomach twists. I swallow.

"I was called by Child Protection once."

Jace's body tenses beside me.

"We were going through a rough patch. Archie's incontinence was worse. I had someone helping in the mornings, and things got mixed up. His lunch-box wasn't refilled. His clothes were washed but some stubborn marks were missed. The school reported it. I was terrified. And angry they didn't talk to me first."

"That's wrong," Tom says.

"It needed addressing," I admit. "But it could have been handled better."

I look around the room. Every face mirrors the same truth.

No one here wants to fight. No one wants to be political. No one wants to be angry.

They just want support without being treated like suspects. They want help without being made scapegoats. They want to raise their children without being blamed for needing what any parent in their situation would need.

They want a system that sees them — not as problems, not as rorters, not as people trying to "get away with something" — but as parents doing the hardest job they never asked for, with love that never runs out and energy that absolutely does.

As the group ends, we all know the truth:

We may not be able to change the NDIS. We may not be able to change the government. Not with everything else we're carrying.

But at least — we have each other.

I just hope that's true with Jace. I don't need him to help with the children — I've coped for this long on my own — but I'm getting attached, and that scares me. Part of me is numb and bracing for it all to fall apart, and the other part wants to confront him and demand answers. This is why so many relationships fizzle in the first weeks or months for me: I need constant assurance that we're okay, that the relationship is going well, that he hasn't lost interest.

I used to get angry at myself, annoyed at this needy side of me. It took me a long time to realise it wasn't because I was needy. It's because I can't read the relationship. I'm the kind of person who is all or nothing, and it's so hard to come back from giving everything only to realise there's nothing on the other side.

He reached for my hand, squeezed it, and held it under the table. It was the sweet gestures that gave me hope. Sure, we kissed, cuddled, and did all the things you'd expect when dating — but I've had that before, and it meant nothing.

But this? This quiet comfort? It meant everything.

Chapter Forty-One

The Deathly Silence

Communication only works when you feel safe enough to ask. People call it insecurity when you ask for reassurance, but it's really a test of safety. You're not afraid of the answer — you're afraid of being judged for having to ask.

Mickey's Blog Bits

Jace

Two weeks later.

Two weeks since movie night. Two weeks since Kayla stepped back from my kiss. Two weeks since something shifted — quietly, invisibly — and I've been trying to pretend I don't feel it.

We still see each other. We still have dinners with Liam and Anna, or with Violet and Archie. We still sit beside each other at parent group. We still talk — easily, even. She laughs at my jokes.

She's my best friend. I don't say that out loud, but it's true. She's the one I want beside me. The one I miss when she pulls away.

But lately her laugh sounds like something she practiced in the mirror — warm at the edges, hollow in the centre. She asks about my day. She remembers the little things. I've kissed her passionately and held her tight and she hasn't pulled away again.

But something's changed.

She's there... but not *open*. Present... but not *reachable*. Warm... but behind a wall I can't see through.

Not cold. Not angry. Just... guarded.

All the parents are struggling I know that. But it's like she's holding herself together with careful hands.

Sometimes she looks at me with this expression — soft, searching, almost longing — like she's waiting for me to say something I don't know I'm supposed to say.

And then there's the times when I try to get close and she steps back just enough that I feel it.

Politely. Gently. But unmistakably.

I've been busy too — trying to figure out what my life looks like now that I plan to try to stay in Australia.

I turned down Seattle yesterday.

I wanted to tell her. I really did. But I kept holding back — not because I didn't trust her, but because I didn't want to get her hopes up. I turned down a high six-figure job in Seattle. The job here in Perth won't come close to that. And until I know my visa is actually going to work out, I can't promise her anything.

I didn't want her to think I was staying for her if staying wasn't possible. I didn't want to hand her hope I couldn't guarantee.

I wanted to tell her once I knew I could stay. Once I had something real. Once the surprise wouldn't hurt her.

But today... Today I felt a flicker of doubt. A tiny, sharp sting.

I pushed it away immediately.

My life should be here. I want my life to be here. I just want Kayla in it.

I call her for the third time this morning.

She finally answers.

Her voice is calm, but thinner than usual. "Hello."

"Hey, Kayla... I was hoping to talk to you." I try to keep my tone light. "Maybe dinner tonight? I'm starting a new job in two weeks, and I wanted to talk to you before I did."

A pause.

Then she shifts — not away from me, but inward.

"A new job — that's exciting," she says, her tone clipped at the edges. "Archie has been struggling all day. I don't think it would be a good time to go out. I would suggest you come here, but I don't know if we'll get a chance to talk. Parent group is on Monday... if you're there, maybe we can talk after. You can tell me about the job."

I thought I could hear something different in her voice when she said the word *job* — like it pained her to say it, which is ridiculous, and probably just me being exhausted. But it did sound like she was trying to sound happy for me, even though something in her tone was tight, stretched thin.

She said Archie had a bad day. That's probably it.

"I don't think I'll be there. I have to fly out of the country—"

I'm cut off mid-sentence as Harry slams into my legs.

"Iz dob, on kuh, Jay!"

"Yes, Harry, I'm talking to Kayla—" I try to gently push him back when I hear Kayla's voice through the phone.

"Jace, I have to go. Talk to you soon."

The line goes dead.

Damn it.

I take a deep breath, trying not to let my frustration show.

"Harry, I needed to talk to Kayla. When I'm on the phone, you can't interrupt."

"Soh-ee, On kuh."

He pushes the phone back up toward my face. "Tah."

Talk.

The one thing we actually need.

My chest tightens.

I can't escape the feeling that she's slipping away. Not running — just... drifting. Quietly. Carefully. Like she's protecting herself from something I can't see.

Maybe she doesn't feel the same way anymore. Maybe she realised she made a mistake. Maybe she's already halfway out the door and I'm the only one who hasn't accepted it.

Hurt flickers first. Then confusion. Then something sharper.

A quiet, heavy ache.

She demanded honesty. She made it a rule. She made it the foundation of us.

And now she's the one keeping something from me.

And I don't know how to reach her through the silence.

One thing is for sure; I want to be at the parent group to talk to her. I immediately get on my phone and start rearranging my flight to leave as soon as possible. I need to leave the country and re -enter to sort out my visa, then I can get back and sort things out with Kayla.

Chapter Forty-Two

What You Don't See

Everyone thinks they know you because they see the outside. But the real story is the one you never say — the one behind your eyes, behind your mask, behind the version of you the world finds easiest to understand.

Mickey's Blog Bits

Kayla

The community centre is buzzing when I arrive — louder, fuller, more chaotic than usual. Chairs are set up in rows instead of the usual circle. There's a table of snacks. A sign-in sheet. A stack of pamphlets.

It feels like a school assembly, not our quiet little parent group.

I slip into the corner — the one spot where no one ever notices me unless they're looking. Liam and Anna walk in together, talking, happy. Liam's home for the week.

Then I see Jace.

My heart starts to race.

Why is he here? I felt gutted when he said he was flying out of the country. He was going to accept the job and he hadn't even told me. I cried for so long. Once I had cried myself numb, I told myself today would be easier if he wasn't here.

Here I was, going out on a limb again. Why? Why do I do this? I learnt early in life that the world could not understand me. Why did I have to have these moments where I let myself be big? Where I let myself stand out? It cost too much! Too much of my soul and my peace. But I wasn't born to be small. God, how I wished I was, that I could hide in the background and be ignored. Something inside me always drove me to something larger, bigger, louder and more prominent. But if this is destiny or purpose – it chose the wrong person.

I follow their movements. He looks stressed too. Maybe something is wrong with the job. Is it too selfish to wish that it fell through? I internally chastise myself.

They don't see me.

I breathe deeply. I can't focus on them right now.

The room is full — more people than usual.

Of course it is.

Today is the "special event."

They've combined all the parent groups together because Mickey from *Our Autistic Journey* is speaking.

Martha spots me and waves me over, her face bright. We've been good since the outburst — better, even. But I shake my head gently, letting her know I'm fine where I am. She nods and turns back to her conversation.

Angela steps to the front.

"Alright everyone, thank you for coming. Today we have a guest speaker — someone many of you know from her writing..."

My stomach flips. The edges of the room feel too bright, too loud — like everything is happening half a second ahead of me.

Time to move.

I walk toward the group, and that's when I see the faces.

Sarah looks at me, then at everyone else, confusion flickering across her features.

Tom and Janette look worried — like they think I'm about to say something that could cause an explosion. They keep glancing at Martha, who looks like she's holding her breath.

Anna and Liam exchange a look.

Jace looks... perplexed.

Priya has a smirk that says *I knew it.*

Of course she did.

I step forward.

"Hey everyone," I say, voice steady even though my heart is pounding. "I am Mikayla 'Mickey' Nukara."

Shock ripples through the room.

Our group gasps. A few hands over mouths. A few whispering, *No way.*

Except for Priya and Angela — they don't even blink.

My eyes flick to Jace — his expression isn't shock, exactly. More like something heavy just clicked into place.

"Some of you know me as Kayla."

"When I started my blog, I was just coming to terms with the autism diagnosis of my kids and myself. I went online and even autistic people were tearing into other autistic people for not talking about autism the 'right' way."

I take a breath.

"To protect my children and myself, I used pseudonyms. And I ask that you continue to use those pseudonyms if you talk about the blog."

The room is silent.

"I look at my life — at my story — and it feels like a soap opera. I've experienced a lot, but I am no victim. I don't tell my story for sympathy or recognition. I write it hoping that something I've been through, or something I've learned, might help someone else."

I shift my weight, grounding myself. I see Martha smiling through tears in my peripheral vision.

"Today I want to open up this session for questions, ideas, strategies — whatever helps. But before I do..."

I swallow.

“I hear people talk about my posts like I’m some guru. Some expert. I’m not. I’m just a parent who’s walked through some tough things with the motto: get back up, reflect, strategise, move forward.”

My voice softens.

“My posts are a way for me to be open in a way I can’t in the rest of my life. I learned to mask early. I learned to protect myself. To survive. And I don’t always know how to turn that off.”

I look directly at Jace as I say it.

“I have always cared too much, too deeply, and that causes a lot of pain. My stories are a reflection of my life circumstances as much as my diagnoses — my trauma, my upbringing, and my responses to challenges.”

Across the room, Jace goes very still. The confusion I'd seen earlier is gone. In its place is something softer. Something that looks dangerously close to understanding.

I have to look away.

“I’m as flawed as anyone else. Please don’t put my stories or opinions on a pedestal.”

I continue, steady now.

“If you’ve read my blogs, you know what I advocate for most: Firstly, just because two autistic people stand next to each other doesn’t mean they think the same, react the same, or are the same. Secondly, high masking doesn’t mean low needs. Level 3 doesn’t mean no independence. Thirdly, we need to listen to as many autistic stories as we can, because we are all different. and lastly – though perhaps most importantly – being a parent of a child with a disability is filled with moments of great beauty, love and joy, but it's also isolating, exhausting and devalued by society and that needs to change."

"We all know and I'm sure wish we didn't have to deal with the current political and media agendas which are trying to paint parents as the unreasonable ones when it comes to disability funding. It couldn't possibly be the bureaucracy killing the smaller providers or the powerful providers making massive profits that are the problem. But I say this not to get political, but to point out that we need each other. Yeah, we rarely have anything else to give, but we can reduce our isolation and share the strategies and the supports that make a difference. I know in my experience that has been really important."

A nervous laugh escapes me.

“Well... that’s enough of my soap box. Over to you.”

Hands fly up everywhere.

I feel like a schoolteacher with a class — it's unnerving, but I push through.

There are the typical questions to begin with, and then—

"Someone told me I should ask autistic people how autism affects them. Do you agree?" a shy woman from the back asks.

"The idea is sound," I say, "but it expects that the autistic person has already come to understand the impact of their autism and can communicate it. It's best to push aside stereotypes in every interaction — with anyone, diagnosis or not. For example, if you're somewhere loud and crowded with a group that includes an autistic person, ask the whole group if it's too loud or crowded. You may be surprised — the autistic person may be fine, and one of your other friends may not be. or when someone around you has an outburst – don't assume it's a tantrum or they are doing it to hurt you. If we're more considerate of everyone and their differences, we'll create a world that naturally becomes more considerate of autistic people. Again, that's my opinion — and you should listen to other autistic voices before forming yours."

A man from the front asks, "I told my friend my daughter was diagnosed autistic, and she said oh we are all a little bit autistic aren't we. I was angered by the comment but I'm not sure if I was wrong."

"People often think they are being considerate or understanding with comments like that, but they don't realise how much that diminishes our struggles. Many people champion autism as a neurotype, downplaying or removing the disability; others call it a superpower, and some try to be sympathetic by relating to what they see as shared experiences. Most have the best of intentions, but they are removing the individual challenges and voices with such overarching and often misguided comments. Yes, autism is in part a neurotype, and if you are lucky enough to live in a society that supports you to the point that you don't experience the impact of the disability side of autism, then that's great — but don't speak for the rest of us who aren't that lucky. Yes, some features of autism — the attention to detail and hyperfocus — may seem to you like a superpower, but again, don't replace our voice and our experiences. And finally, to your point, assuming that my experience is the same as theirs, or experienced at the same level of intensity with the same level of ability to control it, is at best naive and at worst wilfully ignorant. You are not wrong to be annoyed by a comment that, though probably unintentionally, diminished your daughter's voice and experiences."

The rest of the session blurs.

Questions. Stories. People sharing strategies. People thanking me. People crying. People hugging me. People asking for advice I don't feel qualified to give. Directing them to therapists where needed.

Then one question hit my rawest nerve. A man who looked to be in his 20's asked a question that is clearly difficult for him, "Do you think Autistic people can be in loving relationships." I froze. My heart beat loudly in my chest, so loudly I could hear the thump in my ears. I take a deep breath, fighting with everything in me not to look at Jace. My fingernails bite into my palms as I try to hold myself together. "This is probably not a good question for me to ask, I am terrible at relationships."

Across the room people laughed and nodded, murmurings of shared experience heard in pockets of the room. I pushed on, knowing a lot of people here needed the answer as much as the young man who had asked the question. "I have seen strong autistic relationships, and I have seen autistic people struggle with relationships. I believe it's likely that when a person can't accept your autism and its impact on a relationship that will cause strain. Not to treat this too lightly but snoring or different parenting styles can too. I will say that I think my struggle with relationships is more greatly impacted by trauma than anything else. Yes, I really struggle reading the social cues that indicate how to react in the early stages of relationships, but my biggest difficulties come from a desperate need to feel loved and accepted. My childhood taught me that you only get that when you give your all to someone and ask nothing in return. I have spent a lot of time working on that in therapy. If a relationship is important to you and you're struggling its good to talk to a neuro-affirming therapist and have them support you. But don't let people tell you that because you are autistic you will likely never have a relationship."

I saw a grateful smile on the young man's face and a young girl near him seemed very interested. I suspected he would be just fine.

I swept my gaze across the room, ostensibly looking for the next question.

Really, I wanted one glance at Jace.

He was leaning so far forward in his chair it looked like he might face-plant into the floor at any second.

My stomach flipped.

But I couldn't bring myself to meet his eyes.

Not after everything I'd overheard.

Not after everything I'd just revealed.

The next question pulls me back to the room before I can spiral too far. Before I can turn into a humiliated-but-weirdly-proud puddle in front of fifty people.

So I answer it. Then the next one. And the next.

By the time it's over, I'm exhausted.

I step back, relieved it's done — I mouth to Angela, *"Never again"* — and then I see him.

Jace.

Standing beside Anna and Liam.

Hurt. Concerned. Disappointed. Something else I couldn't place.

I don't know what his face is showing — I've never been good with facial expressions, and there has been too much going on today for me to apply context and all the other puzzle pieces I use to understand people.

I hadn't expected him to be here.

I hadn't prepared for this.

He steps forward slightly, eyes searching mine.

I panic.

"I thought you were flying out of the country to your new job coaching in America,"

The words spill out before I can stop them — the fear I've been swallowing for weeks finally breaking the surface.

His face shifts — shock, then anger — *Not a*t me. At Anna. At the situation. At the fact that this is how he found out I knew.

Someone calls my name from across the room.

I grab the lifeline.

"Sorry — I need to..."

I gesture vaguely and slip away before he can say anything.

I don't look back.

I can't. Not yet.

Chapter Forty-Three

Ice Heart

Sometimes you need distance not to pull away, but to see clearly. Reflection isn't coldness — it's the quiet work of making sure you don't bleed old wounds into new love.

Mickey's Blog Bits

Jace

The day after.

The rink is quiet — just the hum of the compressors and the scrape of my blades cutting into the ice. Lap after lap. Turn after turn. Breath in, breath out.

It's the only place my head slows down enough for me to think straight.

My therapist session ended an hour ago, and I've been skating ever since — forty-five minutes of circling the rink like I'm trying to outrun my own thoughts.

I spent the whole session talking about yesterday. About Kayla. About Mickey. About everything I didn't see coming.

I haven't reached out to her. Not yet.

Liam told me to take time to process so I don't say something I regret. I told him that was stupid — I wanted to apologise, clear the air, fix it.

He just looked at me and said, "And what about the fact that she's Mickey?"

I snapped before I could stop myself. "I love her. Mikayla or Kayla — I don't care."

He didn't even blink. "Yeah. But are you ready to reassure her of that?"

I opened my mouth to argue... and nothing came out.

"When did you get so wise?" I muttered.

"About five years into marriage," he said.

I laughed.

But the truth hit hard.

I'm not just dealing with a misunderstanding. I'm dealing with a woman who's spent her whole life expecting people to leave. A woman who masks so well she didn't think she was allowed to tell me who she really was. A woman who overheard something that confirmed her worst fear — that I was leaving and hadn't told her.

And I didn't tell her.
Not because I didn't trust her. Not because I didn't care.

Because I didn't want to mess up something that felt new and fragile and good.

I didn't want the job. I didn't want Seattle. I wanted her.

But I didn't say that. I didn't say anything.

Mark said she probably filled in the silence with every wound she's ever carried.

I push harder, skating faster, the cold air burning my lungs.

Why didn't she tell me she was angry? Why didn't she ask? Why didn't she say anything?

I stop myself — physically and mentally — like sliding into a shot. My knees and hip groaning, echoing the discomfort in my mind.

Do I even get to ask that?

Then I realise she wasn't angry. She was terrified. And I didn't see it.

It wouldn't have happened if I'd told her how I was processing the job offer. If I'd trusted her with the messy parts. If I'd let her see the uncertainty instead of pretending I had everything sorted.

I straighten and start skating backward.

Why didn't she tell me she was Mickey? Why not say she was the woman whose words saved Martha's daughter?

She didn't tell me she was the writer pouring her soul onto the internet while hiding it from everyone in her real life.

I didn't tell her about the job because I didn't want to derail us.

I turn, skating forward again.

Maybe she didn't tell me about Mickey for the same reason. Maybe we're both guilty of protecting something we were terrified to lose.

Because telling me would've meant trusting me with the most vulnerable part of her life — the part she hides from everyone.

I slow down, gliding to a stop at centre ice.

The rink is empty. The world is quiet. And for the first time in two weeks, my mind is too.

I know what I want. I know what's true.

I love her.

Not the idea of her. Not the version she shows the world. Not the mask.

Her.

Kayla. Mikayla. Mickey.

All of her. Every messy, brilliant, wounded, extraordinary part.

I skate to the edge, pull off my gloves, and sit on the bench, breathing hard.

I know what I have to do. I just hope it isn't too late.

My phone buzzes beside me on the bench.

Mel.

For a moment, I consider letting it go to voicemail — not out of resentment, just fatigue — but something in me says answer.

"Hey," I say.

Her voice is lighter than I've heard it in years. "Jace. I just wanted to say thank you. For helping my brother. He's... doing better. Really better. And I wouldn't have managed it without you."

I rub a hand over my face. "I'm glad he's okay."

"And... I met someone," she adds, almost shy. "You were right. I can feel the difference. How he sees me. How we are. It's nothing like... us."

There's no accusation. No nostalgia. Just honesty.

"That's good, Mel," I say. And I mean it.

"I hope things work out for you too," she says softly.

We hang up.

I sit there for a long moment, staring at the ice.

I didn't tell Kayla about this either — about helping Mel's brother, about the late-night calls that weren't about romance but responsibility. It was nothing to me. But that doesn't mean it was nothing to someone else. Anna was right to question it.

Therapy with Mark is helping so much. It's helped me grieve the life I thought I wanted and see the opportunities I have now. It's helped me understand what happened with Liam and Anna – that they didn't want me to leave, that I'm not useless to them. And now I can see the same pattern with Kayla.

Silence isn't neutral. Silence leaves space for fear to grow.

That's why she requested honesty about how I was feeling about the relationship.

And I'm done letting silence do the talking for me.

Chapter Forty-Four

Trigger Warning: Autism, Trauma and Mum

Trigger Warning-

Childhood Narcissistic Abuse

This chapter and the next is not designed to be skipped as it is central to the main character Kayla letting go of her past.
Kayla makes references to the impact on her childhood of her mother's narcissism.
If this is too triggering for you. I will place a basic summary on the key plot points of this chapter and the next without the trigger references at the end of the novel and you can skip the chapter – read the plot points and move to chapter 42

Mickey's Blog – Autism, Trauma, and Mum

I've had a few people message me asking about the relationship between trauma and autism. So let me start with this: **I am not an expert.** I'm just someone who has lived both — deeply, personally, and for a very long time.

Here's what people often forget: **Trauma can mimic autism.** Kids who experience trauma early in life can show behaviours that look autistic — sensory overwhelm, shutdowns, avoidance, rigidity. And with the right therapy and safety, those trauma-based behaviours can fade. That's one of the ways professionals tell the difference.

But you can also have **both**. And that's where things get messy.

I talk about autism and trauma a lot because I've been diagnosed with both. I was born autistic. My father is autistic. My children are autistic. As far as I understand it, there's a very clear genetic line running straight through us — the Autism Family Tree™. My autism diagnosis didn't surprise me.

My trauma diagnosis did.

And here's where people get confused, so let me spell it out clearly:

Autism is my wiring. Trauma is what happened to my wiring. They are not the same thing.

Autism affects how I process the world — sensory load, communication, routines, transitions, executive functioning. Trauma affects how my nervous system responds to danger — hypervigilance, shutdown, dissociation, fawning, fear.

One is developmental. One is experiential. One is lifelong. One is learned. One is neutral. One is painful.

They overlap sometimes, sure. They can look similar from the outside. But inside? They feel completely different. Autism overwhelm is "too much input." Trauma overwhelm is "I'm not safe."

And when you have both, like I am, you learn to tell the difference the hard way.

And so this is where my mum becomes relevant.

By all accounts, I had a good life. Two parents who loved each other despite their dysfunction, a home, food, clothing, stability — all the basics were there. But like many autistic kids, I was emotionally and socially vulnerable in ways nobody recognised. I felt everything too deeply, noticed everything too sharply, and absorbed every tone, every shift, every silence.

And even as a child, I knew my mum was unstable. And my dad? He served daily "critical realism" — which is a polite way of saying he told you the truth whether you wanted it or not.

My love language is affirmation and pebbling. Let's just say I didn't get much of either.

I remember telling therapists over the years that I thought my mum might have been bipolar. It was the only framework I had. But nothing prepared me for the day my trauma therapist — the one guiding me through schema therapy — gently suggested that my mother might actually be a narcissist.

I immediately defended her. I even joked about how we always called Dad the narcissist, but we knew he wasn't — because despite his flaws, Dad would do anything for anyone. Acts of service were his love language. He's not selfish; he's just blunt and wired differently.

I spent weeks defending Mum while simultaneously reading journal articles on narcissism to prove my therapist wrong. But the more I read, the more I realised something I did *not* want to realise:

Not only was my mum a narcissist — but every part of my life, and most of my trauma, had been shaped by her narcissism.

She controlled the whole family, though you'd never have known it. And through that control, the most damaging, influential parts of my life unfolded.

I remember the moment I finally accepted it. It was like a weight of self-hatred slid off my shoulders. I realised that every time I criticised myself, it was *her* voice I heard — not mine.

But accepting the truth doesn't magically free you from it. Surviving that childhood meant I built a whole collection of maladaptive habits — coping strategies that kept me alive then but trip me up now. They're deeply ingrained, automatic, and stubborn. It will take time to unlearn them. Probably a long time. But at least now I know what I'm fighting.

And you're probably wondering why I "let my Dad off" and not my mum.

Simple. Everyone already knew Dad was flawed. His flaws were loud, obvious, and we dealt with the fallout early in life. I also know Dad's history and his neurodivergence. I know what shaped him. And every day — though he'd rather swallow nails than admit it — I see him trying to change.

My mum, on the other hand, would never accept a flaw without turning it back on you. There's a huge difference.

Dad's mistakes hurt, but they weren't manipulative. Mum's mistakes *rewrote reality*.

Dad's flaws were survivable. Mum's were foundational.

Dad’s behaviour was human. Mum’s behaviour was controlling.

And once I saw that clearly — once I understood how her narcissism braided itself through my autism and my trauma — everything finally made sense.

I love my Mum and i always will, but that doesn't change what was.

Chapter Forty-Five

Time to let go

Because of You by Kelly Clarkson, David Hodges and Ben Moody is a song I've wrestled with for years. When I was younger, I heard it as a song of blame — a daughter pointing a finger at her parent. Now I hear it differently. Now it feels like a song about inconvenient truth. A child forced to carry stories meant for adults. A child who became the emotional dumping ground for a parent who should have known better. A child who grew up believing that fear, responsibility and silence were normal. When the singer says she's damaged because of her childhood, it doesn't matter whether people call it "blame" or not — it's truth. And it's a truth I would never place on my own children. Listen to Because of You and decide for yourself.

Mickey's Blog Bits

Kayla

There is a tempest inside me as I stare down at my mum's resting place.

Anger. Sadness. Bitterness. Love. Pity. Sympathy.

All of it swirling, none of it settling.

I'm a fighter — I always have been — but right now I'm frozen. Every instinct in my body is screaming at me to run.

But I came here for a reason. To move forward. To stop carrying the weight of a ghost who still lives in my head.

I force myself to breathe.

Five things I can see.

Four things I can touch.

Three things I can hear.

Two things I can smell.

One thing I can taste.

Deep breath in.

Deep breath out.

"Hey Mum."

My voice cracks on the second word.

"It's crazy that even now it's so hard to be honest with you. To tell you how you hurt me. There's a part of my mind screaming, *'How can you criticise her now that she can't defend herself?'* And another part saying, *'You know it was impossible when she was alive. You would've been the villain and she would've been the victim. Everything would've been twisted until you doubted your own reality.'*"

But I'm not speaking to the woman in the ground. I'm speaking to the echo of you that still tries to run my life.

My hands are trembling. My throat is tight.

I still can't help defending her — even now.

"But I need to confront you, Mum. For my sake."

My body wants to bolt. My brain wants to shut down. But my gut knows I need to do this.

"Mum... you were emotionally immature."

The words feel like broken glass in my mouth.

"Anything you couldn't handle, you projected onto us — long before we could comprehend or carry the weight of your emotional baggage. You shared intimate details of the physical and sexual abuse of children I knew. You told me about your fights with Dad when I was ten. I wasn't there to be your sounding board."

Anger rises — hot, sharp, familiar.

"I wasn't there to be your friend. I was a confused, hurting child. An undiagnosed autistic kid with ADHD who had just lived through early puberty and looked sixteen. The whole world demanded things from me I couldn't give. Did you ever once look at me and think about what I might need?"

The anger breaks through.

"I became a shadow of myself because of you, Mum. I freaked out if my clothes weren't plain. I hid in corners. I did anything to avoid attention — because attention never meant love or pride. It meant danger."

My voice shakes.

"You filled me with fear. Fear of the world outside our family. Fear of people. And that perfect family image you projected — the emotional manipulation, the performance — it sucked the life out of me. It took me decades to break free."

My breath stutters.

Five things I see.

Four things I touch.

Three things I hear.

The anger settles enough for logic to return.

"I know you were mentally unwell."

"I know you were enabled. I know there were excuses — excuses I was taught to believe and repeat. And those excuses didn't just harm me. They harmed you too."

I pause.

"I don't know if things would've been different if people had confronted you. But I won't live the rest of my life filled with unresolved anger, hatred, and blame."

My voice softens.

"You lost out, Mum. You never got to see who I became when I broke free of your hold."

A small, sad smile touches my lips.

“If you could see Violet now... beautiful, confident, free. Watching her take on the world in her own way brings me so much joy and courage. You’ll never see that, Mum. You’ll never see what someone becomes when you stop trying to control them.”

I exhale shakily.

“It was so hard at first not to repeat your voice. To let her dance, be noticed, be loud, be bright. Every time she stood out, a part of me panicked — the part you built. The part that believed hiding was safety. But I had to tear that part down so she could be innocent and free.”

“I’ve come so far, Mum.”

“I don’t hate myself anymore. But those years took a toll. Parts of me are still caged and frightened.”

My chest tightens.

“I’ve always believed I wasn’t built for romantic relationships. They fail before they begin. I get a glimpse of interest and I’m already 150% in — and 150% devastated when it never becomes anything.”

My voice breaks.

“I’m terrified of Jace. Terrified of the possibility of a relationship.”

“Romantic relationships suck. They’re confusing. Every other relationship has clear roles and boundaries. But romance requires connection. Intimacy. Give and take.”

I wipe my face.

“And I’ve never met a guy who thought I was worth breaking down the walls for. There are plenty of other fish in the sea. Why fight for the complicated one?”

A bitter laugh escapes.

“This is the one area where the fear still wins. Because this is the one place where I’d have to let someone in — deeply, consistently — and trust they won’t hurt me the way you did.”

My voice drops to a whisper.

“And the truth is... I’ve probably blown it already.”

The sob hits before I can stop it.

Tears stream down my face. My chest aches.

Five things I see.

Four things I touch.

Three things I hear.

Two things I smell.

One thing I taste.

Breath in.

Breath out.

"I should go."

"I was about to say I wish I could've helped you overcome your issues, Mum... but that wasn't my job."

I swallow.

"But I do wish someone could've helped you. I wish you could've felt free too."

I place my hand on the headstone.

For the first time, I feel a burden lift. I stood up for myself. Maybe not to her physically — but to the part of her that still lives in my head.

I straighten.

"I'm giving your voice in my head notice. Because it's time for an eviction."

I turn and walk away — lighter than I've ever been before.

Chapter Forty-Six

Facing the Music

People think the hardest part of love is holding on. But the real courage is showing up after the misunderstanding, after the fear, after the silence — and choosing to stay anyway.

Mickey's Blog Bits

Kayla

He called me last night and asked me to meet him at the Ice Arena, yes ice arena we are fancy here in Perth, no rinks for us. Anna had blurted through the phone behind him that she would watch the kids. So here I stand on Anna's doorstep with Violet hovering behind me and Archie glued to my side.

"Are you sure?" I ask for the third time.

Anna smiles like she's been waiting for this moment. "Go. We've got them." Then after a little hesitation she adds, " Kayla, I'm sorry for creating the misunderstanding between you and Jace."

I sigh. "Please stop saying sorry. Misunderstandings happen. You called me, you explained it, and that's all you could do."

But inside, shame prickles. If I had just asked him...

And that's the whole point, isn't it? This is why I asked him to be honest with me. When you're someone who struggles to read social cues, body language, and facial expressions, you start to feel ridiculous asking for the hundredth time how the relationship is going, or whether they still feel the same way. You start to sound like the perpetually insecure girlfriend who needs constant reassurance, even when nothing is wrong.

If people were simply honest at each stage, I wouldn't have to ask.

The world can judge that however it likes, but it's my reality — one I've carried my whole life, and one I'm still trying to navigate without feeling like I'm too much.

I turn to wave goodbye to the kids and remind them to follow Anna's instructions.

Violet waves a glitter-covered hand. "Bye Mum! Have fun!"

Archie has already barged into the lounge room like he owns the place. I turn back to Anna.

"Has Jace already left?" I ask, nerves twisting in my stomach. "He's not going to make me try to skate again as punishment."

Anna bursts out laughing. "Don't be ridiculous! He has something to show you there. And why would he punish you? He's annoyed at me for filling your head with misunderstandings."

I smile at her, wave and head to the car. As I drive over I can't help but feel anxious. This isn't infatuation. I know that now, but there are a lot of things that are pulling this relationship apart before it can ever become something lasting. I'm terrified. I'm terrified that this might mean I need to uproot my life and the kids' lives for us to stay together, for something not guaranteed to last. I'm terrified that he might give up everything he wants to stay with us and more than anything I'm terrified he won't think I'm worth it. Yeah I still have stuff to work on, because no matter how I try, deep down I still think my worth is tied to other people's acceptance and time. And when I am brushed aside, ignored or left behind – i feel the small sliver of worth that I have built up crumble again. But that is for another session with my counsellor. Tonight, I'm going to try to put the past fears behind me.

I arrive. Slowly get out of the car and shuffle my way towards the entrance. The rink doors are heavier than I remember. I slip inside, hoping to go unnoticed, but the moment I step in, I see him.

The moment he sees me, something in his shoulders drops — like he's been holding his breath for days.

He looks tired.

I probably do too.

"Hey," he says quietly.

"Hey."

We stand there for a moment — suspended between what we were and what we might still be — then he gestures toward the café.

"Let's find a seat."

We sit on opposite ends of the couch.

Not far. Not close. Just... careful.

We talk.

Not in circles. Not in accusations. Not in half-truths.

It comes out raw and unfiltered.

The overheard conversation. Seattle. Why he didn't tell me. Why I didn't ask. Mickey. Masking. Fear. Limerence. My Mum's narcissism. Silence.

How silence feels like abandonment to me. How conflict feels like failure to him. How we both panicked in different directions.

We talk until the tension drains out of the room and leaves something softer behind — understanding.

We don't need to rehash every detail. We just need to know we finally said the things that mattered.

"No more silent wars," Jace says with a serious yet charming smile.

"Agreed. If something scares us, we say it," I add.

"Yes. And if we can't say it to each other," he adds, "we get help," he states surprising me.

"Couples counselling?" I ask.

He nods, then exhales like he's been holding the words for weeks.

"I love you, Kayla. And I told you once I didn't think I was capable of that. But I am. You're the person I would be devastated to be without. So yeah. Couples counselling if we need it."

Something in my chest loosens — a knot I've carried for years, finally giving way.

He leans toward me, his expression softening in that way that always makes me feel seen. His hands come up to cup my face, warm and steady, his thumbs brushing my cheek like he's afraid I might disappear if he isn't gentle enough.

I exhale, the tension slipping out of me as he presses his forehead to mine for a heartbeat, grounding me before he kisses me. The kiss is slow, deliberate — not rushed, not desperate, just full of the kind of affection that makes my ribs ache in the best way.

It feels like a promise. Not of perfection, not of certainty — but of effort, honesty, and choosing each other even when it's hard.

When he pulls back, his hands stay on my face, holding me like he's still afraid to let go. And for the first time in a long time, I don't feel like I'm bracing for impact. I just feel... held.

He shifts, suddenly nervous. I take in a quick breath prepping myself.

"There's something else," he says. "Something good."

My stomach flips. "Okay..."

"I've been working with the ice sports teams," he says. "Helping out. Running drills. Coaching the younger players."

I smile. "That sounds like you."

"It is," he says, and there's a light in his eyes I haven't seen in weeks. "And they offered me a job. A real one. Not Seattle. Here."

My breath catches.

"I'm developing a program to get young people into hockey," he continues. "And I negotiated a specialised stream for kids with disabilities. Sensory-friendly sessions for kids who struggle with movement."

My eyes sting.

"Jace... that's incredible."

He shrugs, but he's glowing. "It feels right. Like I finally found the thing I'm meant to do."

"And you're staying," I whisper.

"I'm staying," he says. "Because this is home. Because I need you and Violet and Archie. Because this is the life I want."

He takes me on a tour of the centre, excitedly telling me about the program he's setting up, and I can't help but admire everything he's doing.

When I pick up Violet and Archie later, Jace is there with me and Archie runs straight to him while Violet gives him a bright, open smile.

"Jace, guess what?" Violet beams. "I made a dragon!"

Archie points at the TV. "Car."

Jace grins. "A dragon and a car? That's a pretty good day."

He tells Violet about an art contest he thinks she should enter, then takes Archie's hand and leads him to the TV to watch the car show.

The scene settles warmly in my chest.

And I know — quietly, certainly — that I love him too.

El -Hope in the Cracks

Epilogue 1

Priya

The smell of smoked brisket hits me before I even reach the backyard. Liam and Jace have gone all-in on this Texas-style BBQ — giant trays of meat, country music, kids running everywhere, and enough cowboy hats to make me question whether we're still in Australia.

I hover near the fence for a moment, taking it all in.

Kayla is laughing.

Really laughing — head back, shoulders loose, the kind of laugh that comes from somewhere deep and newly healed. Jace is beside her, one hand resting lightly on her back, like he's still surprised he's allowed to touch her.

And then I see it.

The ring.

Simple. Elegant. Exactly her.

A warmth spreads through my chest.

After everything she's been through — everything I suspected long before she said it out loud — she deserves this. She deserves someone who sees her, all of her, and stays.

I grab a plate and wander closer, pretending I'm here for the food. (Okay, partly I am. Liam's ribs are ridiculous.)

Kayla spots me and waves, her smile soft and sure. Jace gives me a nod — the kind men give when they're grateful but still figuring out how to say it.

I nod back.

We don't need words.

We've all become close friends. I've watched their whole journey from the sidelines — the attraction, the fear, the silence, the crash, the repair.

And now this.

A new beginning.

I'm happy for them. Truly.

But happiness has a way of brushing up against the places where you still feel jagged and raw.

Jace and Kayla helped me through the hardest parts of my divorce. And in two weeks we'll all be flying to Colorado — Liam and Anna, Kayla and Jace, Sarah and Dave, every kid we collectively own, and me. Jace is going to shadow the disability snow-sports program at Winter Park so he can bring ideas home, and the rest of us are pretending it's a holiday. Honestly, the thought of the kids being supported for even an hour feels like someone handing me oxygen after a year of shallow breaths.

My three kids are scattered across the yard — the seven-year-old trying to referee the three-year-old, while the five-year-old, Dale, sits under the patio umbrella with noise-cancelling headphones, carefully lining up toy cars in perfect rows. He's not a grass-kid. Never has been.

They're good kids. Exhausting, but good.

Still... sometimes I look at families like Kayla's, like Anna's, and wonder what it would feel like to have someone in my corner. Someone who doesn't just expect me to carry everything. Someone who sees the load and lifts it with me. Someone who cares.

I shake the thought away before it can settle.

Today isn't about me.

Across the yard, the older kids have formed their own little universe.

Violet is showing Allira how to braid a friendship bracelet. Alex is explaining something about dragons with the seriousness of a university lecturer. Sarah's son, Ethan, is nodding along, adding facts of his own. And River, Sarah's stepson, is perched between them all, face-painting the little ones.

They look... happy. Like a group that understands each other without needing to explain everything first.

Sarah is watching them too, leaning into her boyfriend — Dave — who has the calm, steady energy of a man who knows how to show up without taking over. He's flipping sausages with one hand and passing Noah a drink with the other. He was thrilled when everyone accepted River without questions, and Sarah adores both of them.

Good for her. She deserves someone who sees her fire and doesn't try to dim it.

We all do.

"MUM!"

The shout slices through the moment. I turn just in time to see my five-year-old sprinting toward the BBQ table with a fistful of sauce packets and the expression of a child about to commit a crime.

"Oh no you don't—"

I drop my plate and run.

Behind me, I hear Kayla laugh. Jace chuckles. Someone yells, "Priya, he's heading for the brisket!"

Of course he is.

I scoop my son up before he can baptise the meat in tomato sauce, and he shrieks with delighted betrayal.

I can't help laughing too.

Maybe my life is chaos. Maybe I'm tired down to my bones. Maybe I'm still figuring out who I am outside of being everything for everyone.

But as I carry my wriggling child back toward the group, something settles in my chest.

I'm not alone. Not really.

And maybe — just maybe — my story is about to begin too.

E2 - The Last Word

Epilogue 2

Mickey

So... yeah. Mickey was me. Kayla.

Hi again.

You probably guessed, didn't you? I tried to make a whole dramatic moment out of it, but honestly, subtle reveals are for people who don't overshare on the internet.

And if you stuck around long enough to figure me out, then you already know the truth I kept tripping over this whole time:

What you don't see in each person is usually the thing that changes everything.

Take me.
Late-diagnosed autistic. Late-diagnosed ADHD. Late-diagnosed CPTSD.
Each one hiding the others, each one making sure I never got the full picture of myself until far too late.

I lived almost ninety percent of my life not knowing why everything felt harder, louder, sharper, or just... off.
And now that I do know, I can finally say it plainly:

I will always struggle to read social cues, facial expressions, body language.
I will always script and rehearse conversations in my head before I speak.

I will always have executive functioning that works like a shopping trolley with one rogue wheel.
I will always be sensory-oblivious until suddenly I'm not — until it hits, and then I'm sensory-sensitive and avoidant all at once.
I will always carry the rubbish left behind from childhood, the echoes that show up when I'm stressed or overwhelmed.

Yes, I can learn strategies.
Yes, I can desensitise, unlearn, rebuild.
But these things — autism, ADHD, CPTSD — they're lifelong companions.
Not flaws. Not failures. Just the truth of how my brain works.

And knowing that now doesn't magically fix anything...
but it does change everything.

Especially for my kids.

Because if there's one thing I want more than anything, it's to make sure they don't spend most of their lives confused about who they are, the way I did.

And I hope you can see it — how wildly different autistic people can be.
Me. Archie. Violet.
Three autistic brains, nothing alike, all cut from the same brilliant, sideways, impossible cloth.
All shaped by our genetics, our experiences, our internal storms and strengths.
All valid. All real. All worth the time it takes to understand.

Especially my Archie.

In a world that is often shallow, take the time to dig deeper, challenge your misconceptions, embrace the complex and the reward will be richer than you could ever imagine.

And if you're ready for your next adventure... well.

Our little group of misfits isn't done yet. Not even close.

.

The Hidden Battles Series -Coming Soon

Hidden Battles Series Book 0.5 — The Debts She Never Owed – Priya

A woman who spent years paying for someone else's negligence finally stops. With a clever lawyer, a paper trail he never expected, and the truth on her side, Priya forces the man who broke her to face the cost of his own choices — and walks away not with nothing, but with justice.

- the financial abuse
- the emotional neglect
- the reclaiming of power
- Justice

Hidden Battles Series Book 2 — The Storm That Found Us - Priya

A blizzard. A missing child. A man who knows how to find people — and how to stay. Two weeks in Winter Park were meant to be a break, until the storm hits and Priya is forced into close quarters with an Australian paramedic and his two kids. When Joshua disappears into the whiteout, she has no choice but to trust the one person she never expected — and discovers that some storms don't break you. They reveal you.

- forced proximity
- survival stakes
- emotional thawing
- the "competent, steady man" foil to her chaos

Hidden Battles Series – YA novels – Book 1 – **The Patterns the Forest Hid -** ***Violet***

A year after the events of ***What You Don't See****, Violet is finally finding her place — with friends who understand her rhythms, her patterns, her quiet brilliance. On a family camping trip, she, Aleia, River, Alex and Arden discover a hidden hideout deep in the forest... and then threatening notes are left inside for River and Alex.*

The teenagers decide to investigate on their own, determined to solve the mystery before the adults turn it into a full-scale emergency.

But when Arden vanishes without a trace, everything changes. The forest stops feeling like a playground. The clues stop feeling like a game. And Violet must use every pattern she sees — and every instinct she's learned to trust — to uncover the truth before it's too late.

- neurodivergent strengths
- autistic socialisation
- escalating stakes
- Mystery genre

Trigger Safe - Plot Summary for Chapter 44 and 45

Summary Chapter 44 – Autism, Trauma, and Mum

This chapter explains how autism and trauma can look similar from the outside but feel very different on the inside. Autism is described as a lifelong way of processing the world — sensory, social, and cognitive. Trauma is explained as something that happens *to* that wiring, shaping the nervous system's response to danger. The writer has both conditions and talks about how they overlap but are not the same.

The chapter then introduces the writer's childhood. On paper, life looked stable: two parents, a home, basic needs met. But as an autistic child who was emotionally sensitive and socially vulnerable, the writer picked up on instability long before anyone else did. Her father was blunt but loving in his own way, while her mother's behaviour was harder to understand.

During trauma therapy, a clinician gently suggested that her mother might have been narcissistic. At first, the writer resisted the idea and tried to disprove it by researching the topic thoroughly. Over time, she realised that many of her lifelong struggles — especially self-criticism and emotional confusion — were shaped by her mother's patterns of control.

Accepting this truth brought relief, but also the recognition that childhood coping strategies had become deeply ingrained habits in adulthood. The writer explains why she views her father differently: his flaws were visible, understandable, and paired with genuine attempts to change. Her mother, however, did not acknowledge faults and often redirected blame.

The chapter ends with a balanced acknowledgement: the writer still loves her mother, but understanding the impact of her behaviour has been essential for healing and for separating autism from trauma.

Summary Chapter 45 – Time to Let Go

In this chapter, Kayla visits her mother's grave to confront the long-term emotional impact her childhood had on her. She reflects on how her mother's behaviour shaped her fears, her self-image, and her difficulty trusting others, especially in romantic relationships.

Kayla acknowledges that her mother struggled with her own mental health and that the adults around her did not intervene in ways that might have helped. She recognises that, as a child, she took on emotional responsibilities she should not have had, and that this affected her development and sense of safety.

During this visit, Kayla realises several key things that matter for the rest of the book:

She understands that her childhood shaped her instinct to hide, mask, and avoid vulnerability. This explains her difficulty trusting Jace and why she reacts strongly to perceived rejection.

She recognises that she has made different choices with her own children. She sees how she has broken harmful patterns and allowed her daughter to grow up confident and free.

She admits to herself that romantic relationships are the area where she still struggles most. She fears being hurt, misunderstood, or abandoned, and this fear influences her behaviour with Jace.

She realises she may have already damaged her relationship with him. This sets up the emotional stakes for the upcoming chapters.

She symbolically releases the influence her mother's voice still has over her. She decides she no longer wants her mother's past behaviour to dictate her present or future.

By the end of the chapter, Kayla leaves the gravesite feeling lighter and more self-aware. This moment becomes a turning point in her personal growth and directly affects how she approaches her relationship with Jace moving forward.

Made in United States
Orlando, FL
04 November 2026

90200946R00157